Raggylug

The Cottontail Rabbit

And

Other Animal Stories

By

Ernest Seton-Thompson

Author of "Wild Animals I have Known," "The Trail of the Sand Hill Stag," &c.

With Pictures by the Author

British Library Cataloguing-in-Publication Data
A catalogue record for this book is available from the
British Library

Ernest Thompson Seton

Ernest Thompson Seton was born on 14th August 1860, in South Shields, County Durham, England. He grew up to be a pioneering author, wildlife artist, founder of the Woodcraft Indians, and one of the originators of the Boy Scouts of America (BSA).

The Seton family emigrated to Canada when Ernest was just six years old, and most of his childhood was consequently spent in Toronto. As a youth, he retreated to the woods to draw and study animals as a way of avoiding his abusive father – a practice which shaped the rest of his adult life. On his twenty-first birthday, Seton's father presented him with a bill for all the expenses connected with his childhood and youth, including the fee charged by the doctor who delivered him. He paid the bill, but never spoke to his father again.

Originally known as Ernest Evan Thompson, Ernest changed his name to Ernest Thompson Seton, believing that Seton had been an important name in his paternal line. He became successful as a writer, artist and naturalist, and moved to New York City to further his career. Seton later lived at 'Wyndygoul', an estate that he built in Cos Cob, a section of Greenwich, Connecticut. After experiencing vandalism by some local youths, Seton invited the young miscreants to his estate for a weekend, where he told them what he claimed were stories of the American Indians and of nature.

After this experience, he formed the Woodcraft Indians (an American youth programme) in 1902 and invited the local youth to join (at first just boys, but later girls as well). The stories that Seton told became a series of articles written for the *Ladies Home Journal*, and were eventually collected in *The Birch Bark Roll of the Woodcraft Indians* in 1906. Seton also met Scouting's founder, Lord Baden-Powell, in 1906. Baden-Powell had read Seton's book of stories, and was greatly intrigued by it. After the pair had met and shared ideas, Baden-Powell went on to found the Scouting movement worldwide, and Seton became vital in the foundation of the Boy Scouts of America (BSA) and was its first Chief Scout (from 1910 – 1915). Despite this large achievement, Seton quickly became embroiled in disputes with the BSA's other founders, Daniel Carter Beard and James E. West.

In addition to disputes about the content of Seton's contributions to the Boy Scout Handbook, conflicts also arose about the suffrage activities of his wife, Grace, and his British citizenship (it being *an American* organization). In his personal life, Seton was married twice. The first time was to Grace Gallatin in 1896, with whom he had one daughter, Ann (who later changed her name to Anya), and secondly to Julia M. Buttree, with whom he adopted an infant daughter, Beulah (who also changed her first name, to Dee). Alongside his work with the Woodcraft Indians and the BSA, Seton also found time to pursue his primary interest – that of nature writing.

Seton was an early pioneer of animal fiction writing, his most popular work being *Wild Animals I Have Known* (1898), which contains the story of his killing of the wolf Lobo. He later became involved in a literary debate known as the nature fakers controversy, after John Burroughs published an article in 1903 in the *Atlantic Monthly* attacking writers of sentimental animal stories. The controversy lasted for four years and included important

American environmental and political figures of the day, including President Theodore Roosevelt. Seton was also associated with the Santa Fe arts and literary community during the mid-1930s and early 1940s, which comprised a group of artists and authors including author and artist Alfred Morang, sculptor and potter Clem Hull, painter Georgia O'Keeffe, painter Randall Davey, painter Raymond Jonson, leader of the Transcendental Painters Group, and artist Eliseo Rodriguez.

In 1931, Seton became a United States citizen. He died on 23rd October, 1946 (aged eighty-six) in Seton Village in northern New Mexico. Seton was cremated in Albuquerque. In 1960, in honour of his 100th birthday and the 350th anniversary of Santa Fe, his daughter Dee and his grandson, Seton Cottier (son of Anya), in a fitting tribute to the man who loved his surrounding countryside so much, scattered his ashes over Seton Village from an airplane.

LOBO, RAG, AND VIXEN

NOTE TO THE READER

These Stories, selected from those published in "Wild Animals I Have Known," are true histories of the animals described, and are intended to show how their lives are lived.

Though the lower animals have no language in the full sense as we understand it, they have a system of sounds, signs, touches, tastes, and smells that answers the purpose of language, and I merely translate this, when necessary, into English.

ERNEST SETON-THOMPSON

144 Fifth Avenue, New York
May 7, 1899

ILLUSTRATIONS

LOBO

THE KING OF CURRUMPAW

LOBO

THE KING OF CURRUMPAW

I

URRUMPAW is a vast cattle range in northern New Mexico. It is a land of rich pastures and teeming flocks and herds, a land of rolling mesas and precious running waters that at length unite in the Currumpaw River, from which the whole region is named. And the king whose despotic power was felt over its entire extent was an old gray wolf.

Old Lobo, or the king, as the Mexicans called him, was the gigantic leader of a remarkable pack of gray wolves, that had ravaged the Currumpaw Valley for a number of years. All the shepherds and ranchmen knew him well, and, wherever he appeared with his trusty band, terror reigned supreme among the cattle, and wrath and despair among their owners. Old Lobo was a giant among wolves, and was cunning and strong in proportion to his size. His voice at night was well-known and easily distinguished from that of any of his fellows. An ordinary wolf might howl half the night about the herdsman's bivouac without attracting more than a passing notice, but when the deep roar of the old king came booming down the cañon, the watcher bestirred himself and prepared to learn in the morning that fresh and serious inroads had been made among the herds.

Old Lobo's band was but a small one. This I never quite understood, for usually, when a wolf rises to the position and power that he had, he attracts a numerous following. It may be that he had as many as he desired, or perhaps his ferocious temper prevented the increase of his pack. Certain is it that Lobo had only five followers during the latter part of his reign. Each of these, however, was a wolf of renown, most of them were above the ordinary size, one in particular, the second in command, was a veritable giant, but even he was far below the leader in size and prowess. Several of the band, besides the two leaders, were especially noted. One of those was a beautiful white wolf, that the Mexicans called Blanca; this was supposed to be a female, possibly Lobo's mate. Another was a yellow

wolf of remarkable swiftness, which, according
to current stories, had, on several occasions,
captured an antelope for the pack.

It will be seen, then, that these wolves were
thoroughly well-known to the cowboys and
shepherds. They were frequently seen and
oftener heard, and their lives were intimately
associated with those of the cattlemen, who
would so gladly have destroyed them. There
was not a stockman on the Currumpaw who
would not readily have given the value of
many steers for the scalp of any one of Lobo's
band, but they seemed to possess charmed
lives, and defied all manner of devices to kill
them. They scorned all hunters, derided all
poisons, and continued, for at least five years, ·
to exact their tribute from the Currumpaw
ranchers to the extent, many said, of a cow
each day. According to this estimate, therefore, the band had killed more than two thousand of the finest stock, for, as was only too
well-known, they selected the best in every
instance.

The old idea that a wolf was constantly in a
starving state, and therefore ready to eat anything, was as far as possible from the truth in
this case, for these freebooters were always
sleek and well-conditioned, and were in fact

most fastidious about what they ate. Any animal that had died from natural causes, or that was diseased or tainted, they would not touch, and they even rejected anything that had been killed by the stockmen. Their choice and daily food was the tenderer part of a fresh-ly killed yearling heifer. An old bull or cow they disdained, and though they occasionally took a young calf or colt, it was quite clear that veal or horseflesh was not their favorite diet. It was also known that they were not fond of mutton, although they often amused themselves by killing sheep. One night in November, 1893, Blanca and the yellow wolf killed two hundred and fifty sheep, apparently for the fun of it, and did not eat an ounce of their flesh.

These are examples of many stories which I might repeat, to show the ravages of this de-structive band. Many new devices for their extinction were tried each year, but still they lived and throve in spite of all the efforts of their foes. A great price was set on Lobo's head, and in consequence poison in a score of subtle forms was put out for him, but he never failed to detect and avoid it. One thing only he feared—that was firearms, and knowing full well that all men in this region carried them, he never was known to attack or face a human being. Indeed, the set policy of his band was to take refuge in flight whenever, in the day-time, a man was descried, no matter at what distance. Lobo's habit of permitting the pack to eat only that which they themselves had killed, was in numerous cases their salvation, and the keenness of his scent to detect the taint of human hands or the poison itself, completed their immunity.

On one occasion, one of the cowboys heard the too familiar rallying-cry of Old Lobo, and stealthily approaching, he found the Currum-paw pack in a hollow, where they had 'round-ed up' a small herd of cattle. Lobo sat apart on a knoll, while Blanca with the rest was en-deavoring to 'cut out' a young cow, which they had selected; but the cattle were standing in a compact mass with their heads outward, and presented to the foe a line of horns, un-broken save when some cow, frightened by a fresh onset of the wolves, tried to retreat into the middle of the herd. It was only by taking advantage of these breaks that the wolves had succeeded at all in wounding the selected cow, but she was far from being disabled, and it seemed that Lobo at length lost patience with his followers, for he left his position on the hill, and, uttering a deep roar, dashed toward the herd. The terrified rank broke at his charge, and he sprang in among them. Then the cattle scattered like the pieces of a bursting bomb. Away went the chosen victim, but ere she had gone twenty-five yards Lobo was upon her. Seizing her by the neck he suddenly held back with all his force and so threw her heavily to the ground. The shock must have been tremendous, for the heifer was thrown heels over head. Lobo also turned a somersault, but immediately recovered himself, and his followers falling on the poor cow, killed her in a few seconds. Lobo took no part in the killing—after having thrown the victim, he seemed to say, "Now, why could not some of you have done that at once without wasting so much time?"

The man now rode up shouting, the wolves as usual retired, and he, having a bottle of strychnine, quickly poisoned the carcass in three places, then went away, knowing they would return to feed, as they had killed the animals themselves. But next morning, on going to look for his expected victims, he found that, although the wolves had eaten the heifer, they had carefully cut out and thrown aside all those parts that had been poisoned.

The dread of this great wolf spread yearly

among the ranchmen, and each year a larger price was set on his head, until at last it reached $1,000, an unparalleled wolf-bounty, surely; many a good man has been hunted down for less. Tempted by the promised reward, a Texan ranger named Tannerey came one day galloping up the cañon of the Currumpaw. He had a superb outfit for wolf-hunting—the best of guns and horses, and a pack of enormous wolf-hounds. Far out on the plains of the Panhandle, he and his dogs had killed many a wolf, and now he never doubted that, within a few days, old Lobo's scalp would dangle at his saddle-bow.

Away they went bravely on their hunt in the gray dawn of a summer morning, and soon the great dogs gave joyous tongue to say that they were already on the track of their quarry. Within two miles, the grizzly band of Currumpaw leaped into view, and the chase grew fast and furious. The part of the wolf-hounds was merely to hold the wolves at bay till the hunter could ride up and shoot them, and this usually was easy on the open plains of Texas ; but here a new feature of the country came into play, and showed how well Lobo had chosen his range ; for the rocky cañons of the Currumpaw and its tributaries intersect the prairies in

every direction. The old wolf at once made
for the nearest of these and by crossing it got
rid of the horsemen. His band then scattered
and thereby scattered the dogs, and when they
reunited at a distant point of course all of the
dogs did not turn up, and the wolves, no longer
outnumbered, turned on their pursuers and
killed or desperately wounded them all. That
night when Tannerey mustered his dogs, only
six of them returned, and of these, two .. .re
terribly lacerated. This hunter made two
other attempts to capture the royal scalp, but
neither of them was more successful than the
first, and on the last occasion his best horse
met its death by a fall; so he gave up the
chase in disgust and went back to Texas, leaving Lobo more than ever the despot of the
region.

Next year, two other hunters appeared, determined to win the promised bounty. Each
believed he could destroy this noted wolf, the
first by means of a newly devised poison, which
was to be laid out in an entirely new manner;
the other a French Canadian, by poison as-
sisted with certain spells and charms, for he
firmly believed that Lobo was a veritable
'loup-garou,' and could not be killed by ordinary means. But cunningly compounded

poisons, charms, and incantations were all of no avail against this grizzly devastator. He made his weekly rounds and daily banquets as aforetime, and before many weeks had passed, Calone and Laloche gave up in despair and went elsewhere to hunt.

In the spring of 1893, after his unsuccessful attempt to capture Lobo, Joe Calone had a humiliating experience, which seems to show that the big wolf simply scorned his enemies, and had absolute confidence in himself. Calone's farm was on a small tributary of the Currumpaw, in a picturesque cañon, and among the rocks of this very cañon, within a thousand yards of the house, old Lobo and his mate selected their den and raised their family that season. There they lived all summer, and killed Joe's cattle, sheep, and dogs, but laughed at all his poisons and traps, and rested securely among the recesses of the cavernous cliffs, while Joe vainly racked his brain for some method of smoking them out, or of reaching them with dynamite. But they escaped entirely unscathed, and continued their ravages as before. "There's where he lived all last summer," said Joe, pointing to the face of the cliff, "and I couldn't do a thing with him. I was like a fool to him."

II

This history, gathered so far from the cow-boys, I found hard to believe until, in the fall of 1893, I made the acquaintance of the wily marauder, and at length came to know him more thoroughly than anyone else. Some years before, in the Bingo days, I had been a wolf-hunter, but my occupations since then had been of another sort, chaining me to stool and desk. I was much in need of a change, and when a friend, who was also a ranch-owner on the Currumpaw, asked me to come to New Mexico and try if I could do anything with this predatory pack, I accepted the invitation and, eager to make the acquaintance of its king, was as soon as possible among the mesas of that region. I spent some time riding about to learn the country, and at intervals, my guide would point to the skeleton of a cow to which the hide still adhered, and remark, " That's some of his work."

It became quite clear to me that, in this rough country, it was useless to think of pur-suing Lobo with hounds and horses, so that poison or traps were the only available expe-dients. At present we had no traps large enough, so I set to work with poison.

1 need not enter into the details of a hundred devices that I employed to circumvent
this 'loup-garou'; there was no combination
of strychnine, arsenic, cyanide, or prussic acid,
that I did not essay ; there was no manner of
flesh that I did not try as bait; but morning
after morning, as I rode forth to learn the result,
I found that all my efforts had been useless.
The old king was too cunning for me. A single instance will show his wonderful sagacity.
Acting on the hint of an old trapper, I melted
some cheese together with the kidney fat of a
freshly killed heifer, stewing it in a china dish,
and cutting it with a bone knife to avoid the
taint of metal. When the mixture was cool, I
cut it into lumps, and making a hole in one
side of each lump, I inserted a large dose of
strychnine and cyanide, contained in a capsule
that was impermeable by any odor; finally I
sealed the holes up with pieces of the cheese
itself. During the whole process, I wore a
pair of gloves steeped in the hot blood of the
heifer, and even avoided breathing on the
baits. When all was ready, I put them in a
raw-hide bag rubbed all over with blood, and
rode forth dragging the liver and kidneys of
the beef at the end of a rope. With this I
made a ten-mile circuit, dropping a bait at

each quarter of a mile, and taking the utmost care, always, not to touch any with my hands.

Lobo, generally, came into this part of the range in the early part of each week, and passed the latter part, it was supposed, around the base of Sierra Grande. This was Monday, and that same evening, as we were about to retire, I heard the deep bass howl of his majesty. On hearing it one of the boys briefly remarked, " There he is, we'll see."

The next morning I went forth, eager to know the result. I soon came on the fresh trail of the robbers, with Lobo in the lead—his track was always easily distinguished. An ordinary wolf's forefoot is 4½ inches long, that of a large wolf 4¾ inches, but Lobo's, as measured a number of times, was 5½ inches from claw to heel; I afterward found that his other proportions were commensurate, for he stood three feet high at the shoulder, and weighed 150 pounds. His trail, therefore, though obscured by those of his followers, was never difficult to trace. The pack had soon found the track of my drag, and as usual followed it. I could see that Lobo had come to the first bait, sniffed about it, and had finally picked it up.

Then I could not conceal my delight. " I've got him at last," I exclaimed ; "'I shall find him stark within a mile," and I galloped on with eager eyes fixed on the great broad track in the dust. It led me to the second bait and that also was gone. How I exulted—I surely have him now and perhaps several of his band. But there was the broad paw-mark still on the drag ; and though I stood in the stirrup and scanned the plain I saw nothing that looked like a dead wolf. Again I followed—to find now that the third bait was gone—and the king-wolf's track led on to the fourth, there to learn that he had not really taken a bait at all, but had merely carried them in his mouth. Then having piled the three on the fourth, he scattered filth over them to express his utter contempt for my devices. After this he left my drag and went about his business with the pack he guarded so effectively.

This is only one of many similar experiences which convinced me that poison would never avail to destroy this robber, and though I continued to use it while awaiting the arrival of the traps, it was only because it was meanwhile a sure means of killing many prairie wolves and other destructive vermin.

About this time there came under my observation an incident that will illustrate Lobo's diabolic cunning. These wolves had at least one pursuit which was merely an amusement, it was stampeding and killing sheep, though they rarely ate them. The sheep are usually kept in flocks of from one thousand to three thousand under one or more shepherds. At night they are gathered in the most sheltered place available, and a herdsman sleeps on each side of the flock to give additional protection. Sheep are such senseless creatures that they are liable to be stampeded by the veriest trifle, but they have deeply ingrained in their nature one, and perhaps only one, strong weakness, namely, to follow their leader. And this the shepherds turn to good account by putting half a dozen goats in the flock of sheep. The latter recognize the superior intelligence of their bearded cousins, and when a night alarm occurs they crowd around them, and usually are thus saved from a stampede and are easily protected. But it was not always so. One night late in last November, two Perico shepherds were aroused by an onset of wolves. Their flocks huddled around the goats, which being neither fools nor cowards, stood their ground and were bravely defiant; but alas for them, no common wolf was heading this attack. Old Lobo, the weir-wolf, knew as well as the shepherds that the goats were the moral force of the flock, so

hastily running over the backs of the densely
packed sheep, he fell on these leaders, slew
them all in a few minutes, and soon had the
luckless sheep stampeding in a thousand different directions. For weeks afterward I was almost daily accosted by some anxious shepherd,
who asked, "Have you seen any stray OTO
sheep lately?" and usually I was obliged to say
I had; one day it was, "Yes, I came on some
five or six carcasses by Diamond Springs;"
or another, it was to the effect that I had seen
a small 'bunch' running on the Malpai Mesa;
or again, "No, but Juan Meira saw about
twenty, freshly killed, on the Cedra Monte
two days ago."

At length the wolf traps arrived, and with
two men I worked a whole week to get them
properly set out. We spared no labor or pains,
I adopted every device I could think of that
might help to insure success. The second day
after the traps arrived, I rode around to inspect, and soon came upon Lobo's trail running
from trap to trap. In the dust I could read the
whole story of his doings that night. He had
trotted along in the darkness, and although the
traps were so carefully concealed, he had instantly detected the first one. Stopping the
onward march of the pack, he had cautiously

scratched around it until he had disclosed the trap, the chain, and the log, then left them wholly exposed to view with the trap still unsprung, and passing on he treated over a dozen traps in the same fashion. Very soon I noticed that he stopped and turned aside as soon as he detected suspicious signs on the trail, and a new plan to outwit him at once suggested itself. I set the traps in the form of an H; that is, with a row of traps on each side of the trail, and one on the trail for the cross-bar of the H. Before long, I had an opportunity to count another failure. Lobo came trotting along the trail, and was fairly between the parallel lines before he detected the single trap in the trail, but he stopped in time, and why and how he knew enough I cannot tell; the Angel of the wild things must have been with him, but without turning an inch to the right or left, he slowly and cautiously backed on his own tracks, putting each paw exactly in its old track until he was off the dangerous ground. Then returning at one side he scratched clods and stones with his hind feet till he had sprung every trap. This he did on many other occasions, and although I varied my methods and redoubled my precautions, he was never deceived, his sagacity seemed never at fault, and he might have

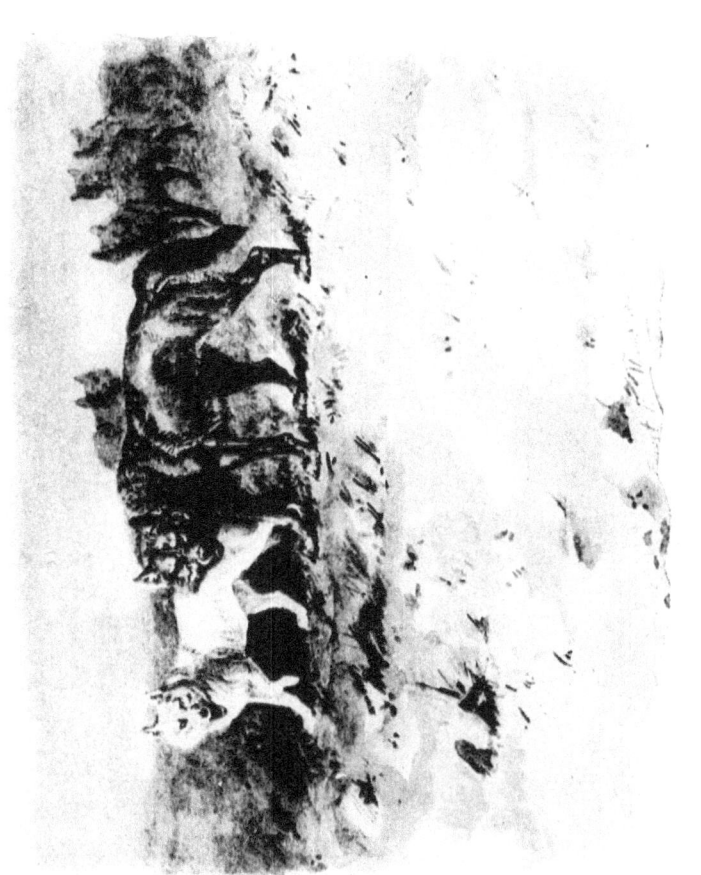

Lobo and Blanca.

been pursuing his career of rapine to-day, but for an unfortunate alliance that proved his ruin and added his name to the long list of heroes who, unassailable when alone, have fallen through the indiscretion of a trusted ally.

III

Once or twice, I had found indications that everything was not quite right in the Currumpaw pack. There were signs of irregularity, I thought; for instance there was clearly the trail of a smaller wolf running ahead of the leader, at times, and this I could not understand until a cowboy made a remark which explained the matter.

" I saw them to-day," he said, "and the wild one that breaks away is Blanca." Then the truth dawned upon me, and I added, " Now, I know that Blanca is a she-wolf, because were a he-wolf to act thus, Lobo would kill him at once."

This suggested a new plan. I killed a heifer, and set one or two rather obvious traps about the carcass. Then cutting off the head, which is considered useless offal, and quite beneath the notice of a wolf, I set it a little apart and around it placed six powerful steel traps properly deodorized and concealed with the utmost care. During my operations I kept my hands, boots, and implements smeared with fresh blood, and afterward sprinkled the ground with the same, as though it had flowed from the head; and when the traps were buried in the dust I brushed the place over with the skin of a coyote, and with a foot of the same animal made a number of tracks over the traps. The head was so placed that there was a narrow passage between it and some tussocks, and in this passage I buried two of my best traps, fastening them to the head itself.

Wolves have the habit of approaching every carcass they get the wind of, in order to examine it, even when they have no intention of eating it, and I hoped that this habit would bring the Currumpaw pack within reach of my latest stratagem. I did not doubt that Lobo would detect my handiwork about the meat, and prevent the pack approaching it, but I did build some hopes on the head, for it looked as though it had been thrown aside as useless.

Next morning, I sallied forth to inspect the traps, and there, oh, joy! were the tracks of the pack, and the place where the beef-head and its traps had been was empty. A hasty study of the trail showed that Lobo had kept the pack from approaching the meat, but one, a small wolf, had evidently gone on to examine the head as it lay apart and had walked right into one of the traps.

We set out on the trail, and within a mile discovered that the hapless wolf was Blanca. Away she went, however, at a gallop, and although encumbered by the beef-head, which weighed over fifty pounds, she speedily distanced my companion who was on foot. But we overtook her when she reached the rocks, for the horns of the cow's head became caught and held her fast. She was the handsomest wolf I had ever seen. Her coat was in perfect condition and nearly white.

She turned to fight, and raising her voice in the rallying cry of her race, sent a long howl rolling over the cañon. From far away upon the mesa came a deep response, the cry of Old Lobo. That was her last call, for now we had closed in on her, and all her energy and breath were devoted to combat.

Then followed the inevitable tragedy, the idea of which I shrank from afterward more than at the time. We each threw a lasso over the neck of the doomed wolf, and strained our horses in opposite directions until the blood burst from her mouth, her eyes glazed, her

limbs stiffened and then fell limp.   Homeward
then we rode, carrying the dead wolf, and ex-
ulting over this, the first death-blow we had
been able to inflict on the Currumpaw pack.

At intervals during the tragedy, and afterward as we rode homeward, we heard the roar
of Lobo as he wandered about on the distant .
mesas, where he seemed to be searching for
Blanca.   He had never really deserted her,
but knowing that he could not save her, his
deep-rooted dread of firearms had been too
much for him when he saw us approaching.
All that day we heard him wailing as he
roamed in his quest, and I remarked at length
to one of the boys, " Now, indeed, I truly know
that Blanca was his mate."

As evening fell he seemed to be coming
toward the home cañon, for his voice sounded
continually nearer.   There was an unmistakable note of sorrow in it now.   It was no longer
the loud, defiant howl, but a long, plaintive
wail: " Blanca! Blanca!" he seemed to call.
And as night came down, I noticed that he
was not far from the place where we had over-
taken her.   At length he seemed to find the
trail, and when he came to the spot where we
had killed her, his heart-broken wailing was
piteous to hear.   It was sadder than I could

possibly have believed. Even the stolid cow-boys noticed it, and said they had "never heard a wolf carry on like that before." He seemed to know exactly what had taken place, for her blood had stained the place of her death.

Then he took up the trail of the horses and followed it to the ranch-house. Whether in hopes of finding her there, or in quest of revenge, I know not, but the latter was what he found, for he surprised our unfortunate watchdog outside and tore him to little bits within fifty yards of the door. He evidently came alone this time, for I found but one trail next morning, and he had galloped about in a reckless manner that was very unusual with him. I had half expected this, and had set a number of additional traps about the pasture. Afterward I found that he had indeed fallen into one of these, but such was his strength, he had torn himself loose and cast it aside.

I believed that he would continue in the neighborhood until he found her body at least, so I concentrated all my energies on this one enterprise of catching him before he left the region, and while yet in this reckless mood. Then I realized what a mistake I had made in killing Blanca, for by using her as a decoy I might have secured him the next night.

I gathered in all the traps I could command, one hundred and thirty strong steel wolf-traps, and set them in fours in every trail that led into the cañon; each trap was separately fastened to a log, and each log was separately buried. In burying them, I carefully removed the sod and every particle of earth that was lifted we put in blankets, so that after the sod was replaced and all was finished the eye could detect no trace of human handiwork. When the traps were concealed I trailed the body of poor Blanca over each place, and made of it a drag that circled all about the ranch, and finally I took off one of her paws and made with it a line of tracks over each trap. Every precaution and device known to me I used, and retired at a late hour to await the result.

Once during the night I thought I heard Old Lobo, but was not sure of it. Next day I rode around, but darkness came on before I completed the circuit of the north cañon, and I had nothing to report. At supper one of the cowboys said, "There was a great row among the cattle in the north cañon this morning, maybe there is something in the traps there." It was afternoon of the next day before I got to the place referred to, and as I drew near a great grizzly form arose from the ground, vainly en-

deavoring to escape, and there revealed before
me stood Lobo, King of the Currumpaw, firmly
held in the traps. Poor old hero, he had never
ceased to search for his darling, and when he
found the trail her body had made he followed
it recklessly, and so fell into the snare prepared
for him. There he lay in the iron grasp of all
four traps, perfectly helpless, and all around him
were numerous tracks showing how the cattle
had gathered about him to insult the fallen despot, without daring to approach within his
reach. For two days and two nights he had
lain there, and now was worn out with struggling. Yet, when I went near him, he rose up
with bristling mane and raised his voice, and
for the last time made the cañon reverberate
with his deep bass roar, a call for help, the
muster call of his band. But there was none
to answer him, and, left alone in his extremity,
he whirled about with all his strength and made
a desperate effort to get at me. All in vain,
each trap was a dead drag of over three hundred pounds, and in their relentless fourfold
grasp, with great steel jaws on every foot, and
the heavy logs and chains all entangled together,
he was absolutely powerless. How his huge
ivory tusks did grind on those cruel chains, and
when I ventured to touch him with my rifle-

barrel he left grooves on it which are there to this day. His eyes glared green with hate and fury, and his jaws snapped with a hollow ' chop,' as he vainly endeavored to reach me and my trembling horse. But he was worn out with hunger and struggling and loss of blood, and he soon sank exhausted to the ground.

Something like compunction came over me, as I prepared to deal out to him that which so many had suffered at his hands.

" Grand old outlaw, hero of a thousand lawless raids, in a few minutes you will be but a great load of carrion. It cannot be otherwise." Then I swung my lasso and sent it whistling over his head. But not so fast; he was yet far from being subdued, and, before the supple coils had fallen on his neck he seized the noose and, with one fierce chop, cut through its hard thick strands, and dropped it in two pieces at his feet.

Of course I had my rifle as a last resource, but I did not wish to spoil his royal hide, so I galloped back to the camp and returned with a cowboy and a fresh lasso. We threw to our victim a stick of wood which he seized in his teeth, and before he could relinquish it our lassoes whistled through the air and tightened on his neck.

Yet before the light had died from his fierce eyes, I cried, " Stay, we will not kill him ; let us take him alive to the camp." He was so completely powerless now that it was easy to put a stout stick through his mouth, behind his tusks, and then lash his jaws with a heavy cord which was also fastened to the stick. The stick kept the cord in, and the cord kept the stick in, so he was harmless. As soon as he felt his jaws were tied he made no further resistance, and uttered no sound, but looked calmly at us and seemed to say, " Well, you have got me at last, do as you please with me." And from that time he took no more notice of us.

We tied his feet securely, but he never groaned, nor growled, nor turned his head. Then with our united strength we were just able to put him on my horse. His breath came evenly as though sleeping, and his eyes were bright and clear again, but did not rest on us. Afar on the great rolling mesas they were fixed, his passing kingdom, where his famous band was now scattered. And he gazed till the pony descended the pathway into the cañon, and the rocks cut off the view.

By travelling slowly we reached the ranch in safety, and after securing him with a collar and a strong chain, we staked him out in the past-

ure and removed the cords.   Then for the first
time I could examine him closely, and proved
how unreliable is vulgar report where a living
hero or tyrant is concerned.   He had *not* a
collar of gold about his neck, nor was there on
his shoulders an inverted cross to denote that
he had leagued himself with Satan.   But I did
find on one haunch a great broad scar, that
tradition says was the fang-mark of Juno, the
leader of Tannerey's wolf-hounds — a mark
which she gave him the moment before he
stretched her lifeless on the sand of the cañon.

I set meat and water beside him, but he paid
no heed. He lay calmly on his breast, and
gazed with those steadfast yellow eyes away
past me down through the gateway of the
cañon, over the open plains—his plains—nor
moved a muscle when I touched him.   When
the sun went down he was still gazing fixedly
across the prairie.   I expected he would call up
his band when night came, and prepared for
them, but he had called once in his extremity,
and none had come; he would never call again.

A lion shorn of his strength, an eagle robbed
of his freedom, or a dove bereft of his mate, all
die, it is said, of a broken heart; and who will

aver that this grim bandit could bear the three-
fold brunt, heart-whole? This only I know,
that when the morning dawned, he was lying
there still in his position of calm repose, but his
spirit was gone—the old king-wolf was dead.

I took the chain from his neck, a cowboy
helped me to carry him to the shed where lay
the remains of Blanca, and as we laid him beside her, the cattle-man exclaimed: "There,
you *would* come to her, now you are together
again."

REDRUFF

THE STORY OF THE DON VALLEY PARTRIDGE

REDRUFF

THE STORY OF THE DON VALLEY PARTRIDGE

I

DOWN the wooded slope of Taylor's Hill the Mother Partridge led her brood; down toward the crystal brook that by some strange whim was called Mud Creek. Her little ones were one day old but already quick on foot, and she was taking them for the first time to drink.

She walked slowly, crouching low as she went, for the woods were full of enemies. She was uttering a soft little cluck in her throat, a call to the little balls of mottled down that on their tiny pink legs came toddling after, and peeping softly and plaintively if left even a few inches behind, and seeming so fragile they made the very chicadees look big and coarse. There were twelve of them, but Mother Grouse watched them all, and she watched every bush and tree and thicket, and the whole woods and the sky itself. Always for enemies she seemed seeking—friends were too scarce to be looked for—and an enemy she found. Away across the level beaver meadow was a great brute of a fox. He was coming their way, and in a few moments would surely wind them or strike their trail. There was no time to lose.

'*Krrr! Krrr!*' (Hide! Hide!) cried the mother in a low, firm voice, and the little bits of things, scarcely bigger than acorns and but a day old, scattered far (a few inches) apart to hide. One dived under a leaf, another between two roots, a third crawled into a curl of birch-bark, a fourth into a hole, and so on, till all were hidden but one who could find no cover, so squatted on a broad yellow chip and lay very flat, and closed his eyes very tight, sure that now he was safe from being seen. They ceased their frightened peeping and all was still.

Mother Partridge flew straight toward the dreaded beast, alighted fearlessly a few yards to one side of him, and then flung herself on the ground, flopping as though winged and lame—oh, so dreadfully lame—and whining like a distressed puppy. Was she begging for mercy—mercy from a bloodthirsty, cruel fox? Oh, dear, no! She was no fool. One often

hears of the cunning of the fox. Wait and see
what a fool he is compared with a mother-par-
tridge. Elated at the prize so suddenly within
his reach, the fox turned with a dash and caught
—at least, no, he didn't quite catch the bird;
she flopped by chance just a foot out of reach.
He followed with another jump and would
have seized her this time surely, but somehow
a sapling came just between, and the partridge
dragged herself awkwardly away and under a
log, but the great brute snapped his jaws and
bounded over the log, while she, seeming a
trifle less lame, made another clumsy forward
spring and tumbled down a bank, and Reynard,
keenly following, almost caught her tail, but,
oddly enough, fast as he went and leaped, she
still seemed just a trifle faster. It was most ex-
traordinary. A winged partridge and he, Reynard, the Swift-foot, had not caught her in five
minutes' racing. It was really shameful. But
the partridge seemed to gain strength as the fox
put forth his, and after a quarter of a mile race,
racing that was somehow all away from Taylor's Hill, the bird got unaccountably quite
well, and, rising with a decisive whirr, flew off
through the woods, leaving the fox utterly dum-
founded to realize that he had been made a fool
of, and, worst of all, he now remembered that

this was not the first time he had been served this very trick, though he never knew the reason for it.

Meanwhile Mother Partridge skimmed in a great circle and came by a roundabout way back to the little fuzz-balls she had left hidden in the woods.

With a wild bird's keen memory for places, she went to the very grass-blade she last trod on, and stood for a moment fondly to admire the perfect stillness of her children. Even at her step not one had stirred, and the little fellow on the chip, not so very badly concealed after all, had not budged, nor did he now ; he only closed his eyes a tiny little bit harder, till the mother said :

'*K-reet!*' (Come, children) and instantly, like a fairy story, every hole gave up its little baby-partridge, and the wee fellow on the chip, the biggest of them all really, opened his big-little eyes and ran to the shelter of her broad tail, with a sweet little '*peep peep*' which an enemy could not have heard three feet away, but which his mother could not have missed thrice as far, and all the other thimblefuls of down joined in, and no doubt thought themselves dreadfully noisy, and were proportionately happy.

The sun was hot now. There was an open space to cross on the road to the water, and, after a careful lookout for enemies, the mother gathered the little things under the shadow of her spread fantail and kept off all danger of sunstroke until they reached the brier thicket by the stream.

Here a cottontail rabbit leaped out and gave them a great scare. But the flag of truce he carried behind was enough. He was an old friend; and among other things the little ones learned that day that Bunny always sails under a flag of truce, and lives up to it too.

And then came the drink, the purest of living water, though silly men had called it Mud Creek.

At first the little fellows didn't know how to drink, but they copied their mother, and soon learned to drink like her and give thanks after every sip. There they stood in a row along the edge, twelve little brown and golden balls on twenty-four little pink-toed, in-turned feet, with twelve sweet little golden heads gravely bowing, drinking, and giving thanks like their mother.

Then she led them by short stages, keeping the cover, to the far side of the beaver-meadow, where was a great, grassy dome. The mother

had made a note of this dome some time before. It takes a number of such domes to raise
a brood of partridges. For this was an ant's
nest. The old one stepped on top, looked
about a moment, then gave half a dozen vigorous rakes with her claws. The friable ant-hill
was broken open, and the earthen galleries
scattered in ruins down the slope. The ants
swarmed out and quarrelled with each other
for lack of a better plan. Some ran around the
hill with vast energy and little purpose, while a
few of the more sensible began to carry away
fat white eggs. But the old partridge, coming
to the little ones, picked up one of these juicy-
looking bags and clucked and dropped it, and
picked it up again and again and clucked, then
swallowed it. The young ones stood around,
then one little yellow fellow, the one that sat on
the chip, picked up an ant-egg, dropped it a
few times, then yielding to a sudden impulse,
swallowed it, and so had learned to eat. Within twenty minutes even the runt had learned,
and a merry time they had scrambling after the
delicious eggs as their mother broke open more
ant-galleries, and sent them and their contents
rolling down the bank, till every little partridge
had so crammed his little crop that he was pos-
itively misshapen and could eat no more.

Then all went cautiously up the stream, and on a sandy bank, well screened by brambles, they lay for all that afternoon, and learned how pleasant it was to feel the cool, powdery dust running between their hot little toes. With their strong bent for copying, they lay on their sides like their mother and scratched with their tiny feet and flopped with their wings, though they had no wings to flop with, only a little tag among the down on each side, to show where the wings would come. That night she took them to a dry thicket near by, and there among the crisp, dead leaves that would prevent an enemy's silent approach on foot, and under the interlacing briers that kept off all foes of the air, she cradled them in their feather-shingled nursery and rejoiced in the fulness of a mother's joy over the wee cuddling things that peeped in their sleep and snuggled so trustfully against her warm body.

II

The third day the chicks were much stronger on their feet. They no longer had to go around an acorn; they could even scramble over pine-cones, and on the little tags that marked the places for their wings, were now to be seen blue rows of fat blood-quills.

Their start in life was a good mother, good legs, a few reliable instincts, and a germ of reason. It was instinct, that is, inherited habit, which taught them to hide at the word from their mother; it was instinct that taught them to follow her, but it was reason which made them keep under the shadow of her tail when the sun was smiting down, and from that day reason entered more and more into their expanding lives.

Next day the blood-quills had sprouted the tips of feathers. On the next, the feathers were well out, and a week later the whole family of down-clad babies were strong on the wing.

And yet not all—poor little Runtie had been sickly from the first. He bore his half-shell on his back for hours after he came out; he ran less and cheeped more than his brothers, and when one evening at the onset of a skunk the mother gave the word ' *Kwit, kwit* ' (Fly, fly), Runtie was left behind, and when she gathered her brood on the piney hill he was missing, and they saw him no more.

Meanwhile, their training had gone on. They knew that the finest grasshoppers abounded in the long grass by the brook; they knew that the currant-bushes dropped fatness in the

form of smooth, green worms; they knew that
the dome of an ant-hill rising against the distant woods stood for a garner of plenty; they
knew that strawberries, though not really insects, were almost as delicious; they knew
that the huge danaid butterflies were good,
safe game, if they could only catch them, and
that a slab of bark dropping from the side of
a rotten log was sure to abound in good things
of many different kinds; and they had learned,
also, the yellow-jackets, mud-wasps, woolly
worms, and hundred-leggers were better let
alone.

It was now July, the Moon of Berries. The
chicks had grown and flourished amazingly
during this last month, and were now so large
that in her efforts to cover them the mother
was kept standing all night.

They took their daily dust-bath, but of late
had changed to another higher on the hill. It
was one in use by many different b:.ds, and at
first the mother disliked the idea of such a
second-hand bath. But the dust was of such
a fine, agreeable quality, and the children led
the way with such enthusiasm, that she forgot
her mistrust.

After a fortnight the little ones began to
droop and she herself did not feel very well.

They were always hungry, and though they
ate enorriously, they one and all grew thinner
and thinner. The mother was the last to be
affected. But when it came, it came as hard
on her—a ravenous hunger, a feverish head-
ache, and a wasting weakness. She never
knew the cause. She could not know that the
dust of the much-used dust-bath, that her true
instinct taught her to mistrust at first, and now
again to shun, was sown with parasitic worms,
and that all of the family were infested.

No natural impulse is without a purpose.
The mother-bird's knowledge of healing was
only to follow natural impulse. The eager,
feverish craving for something, she knew not
what, led her to eat, or try, everything that
looked eatable and to seek the coolest woods.
And there she found a deadly sumach laden
with its poison fruit. A month ago she would
have passed it by, but now she tried the un-
attractive berries. The acrid burning juice
seemed to answer some strange demand of her
body; she ate and ate, and all her family
joined in the strange feast of physic. No human doctor could have hit it better; it proved
a biting, drastic purge, the dreadful secret foe
was downed, the danger passed. But not for
all---Nature, the old nurse, had come too late

for two of them. The weakest, by inexorable law, dropped out. Enfeebled by the disease, the remedy was too severe for them. They drank and drank by the stream, and next morning did not move when the others followed the mother. Strange vengeance was theirs now, for a skunk, the same that could have told where Runtie went, found and devoured their bodies and died of the poison they had eaten.

Seven little partridges now obeyed the mother's call. Their individual characters were early shown and now developed fast. The weaklings were gone, but there was still a fool and a lazy one. The mother could not help caring for some more than for others, and her favorite was the biggest, he who once sat on the yellow chip for concealment. He was not only the biggest, strongest, and handsomest of the brood, the best of all, the most obedient. His mother's warning ' *rrrrr* ' (danger) did not always keep the others from a risky path or a doubtful food, but obedience seemed natural to him, and he never failed to respond to her soft ' *K-reet* ' (Come), and of this obedience he reaped the reward, for his days were longest in the land.

August, the Molting Moon, went by; the

young ones were now three parts grown. They knew just enough to think themselves wonderfully wise. When they were small it was necessary to sleep on the ground so their mother could shelter them, but now they were too big to need that, and the mother began to introduce grown-up ways of life. It was time to roost in the trees. The young weasels, foxes, skunks, and minks were beginning to run. The ground grew more dangerous each night, so at sundown Mother Partridge called ' *K-reet,*' and flew into a thick, low tree.

The little ones followed, except one, an obstinate little fool who persisted in sleeping on the ground as heretofore. It was all right that time, but the next night his brothers were awakened by his cries. There was a slight scuffle, then stillness, broken only by a horrid sound of crunching bones and a smacking of lips. They peered down into the terrible darkness below, where the glint of two close-set eyes and a peculiar musty smell told them that a mink was the killer of their fool brother.

Six little partridges now sat in a row at night, with their mother in the middle, though it was not unusual for some little one with cold feet to perch on her back.

Their education went on, and about this time

they were taught 'whirring.' A partridge can rise on the wing silently if it wishes, but whirring is so important at times that all are taught how and when to rise on thundering wings. Many ends are gained by the whirr. It warns all other partridges near that danger is at hand, it unnerves the gunner, or it fixes the foe's attention on the whirrer, while the others sneak off in silence, or by squatting, escape notice.

A partridge adage might well be 'foes and food for every moon.' September came, with seeds and grain in place of berries and ant-eggs, and gunners in place of skunks and minks.

The partridges knew well what a fox was, but had scarcely seen a dog. A fox they knew they could easily baffle by taking to a tree, but when in the Gunner Moon old Cuddy came prowling through the ravine with his bob-tailed yellow cur, the mother spied the dog and cried out '*Kwit! Kwit!*' (Fly, fly). Two of the brood thought it a pity their mother should lose her wits so easily over a fox, and were pleased to show their superior nerve by springing into a tree in spite of her earnestly repeated '*Kwit! Kwit!*' and her example of speeding away on silent wings.

Meanwhile, the strange bob-tailed fox came under the tree and yapped and yapped at them.

They were much amused at him and at their mother and brothers, so much so that they never noticed a rustling in the bushes till there was a loud *Bang ! bang !* and down 'ell two bloody, flopping partridges, to be seized and mangled by the yellow cur until the gunner ran from the bushes and rescued the remains.

III

Cuddy lived in a wretched shanty near the Don, north of Toronto. His was what Greek philosophy would have demonstrated to be an ideal existence. He had no wealth, no taxes, no social pretensions, and no property to speak of. His life was made up of a very little work and a great deal of play, with as much out-door life as he chose. He considered himself a true sportsman because he was 'fond o' huntin',' and 'took a sight o' comfort out of seein' the critters hit the mud' when his gun was fired. The neighbors called him a squatter, and looked on him merely as an anchored tramp. He shot and trapped the year round, and varied his game somewhat with the season perforce, but had been heard to remark he could tell the month by the 'taste o' the patridges,' if he didn't happen to know by the almanac. This, no doubt, showed keen observation, but was also unfortunate proof of something not so creditable. The lawful season for murdering partridges began September 15th, but there was nothing surprising in Cuddy's be'ng out a fort-night ahead of time. Yet he managed to es-cape punishment year after year, and even con-trived to pose in a newspaper interview as an interesting character.

He rarely shot on the wing, preferring to pot his birds, which was not easy to do when the leaves were on, and accounted for the brood in the third ravine going so long unharmed ; but the near prospect of other gunners finding them now, had stirred him to go after 'a mess of birds.' He had heard no roar of wings when the mother-bird led off her four survivors, so pocketed the two he had killed and returned to the shanty.

The little grouse thus learned that a dog is not a fox, and must be differently played ; and an old lesson was yet more deeply graven— ' Obedience is long life.'

The rest of September was passed in keeping quietly out of the way of gunners as well as some old enemies. They still roosted on the long, thin branches of the hardwood trees among the thickest leaves, which protected them from foes in the air; the height saved them from foes on the ground, and left them nothing to fear but coons, whose slow, heavy tread on the limber boughs never failed to give them timely warning. But the leaves were falling now— every month its foes and its food. This was nut time, and it was owl time, too. Barred owls coming down from the north doubled or trebled the owl population. The nights were getting frosty and the coons less dangerous, so the mother changed the place of roosting to the thickest foliage of a hemlock-tree.

Only one of the brood disregarded the warning '*Kreet, kreet.*' He stuck to his swinging elm-bough, now nearly naked, and a great yellow-eyed owl bore him off before morning.

Mother and three young ones now were left, but they were as big as she was; indeed one, the eldest, he of the chip, was bigger. Their ruffs had begun to show. Just the tips, to tell what they would be like when grown, and not a little proud they were of them.

The ruff is to the partridge what the train is to the peacock—his chief beauty and his pride. A hen's ruff is black with a slight green gloss. A cock's is much larger and blacker and is glossed with more vivid bottle-green. Once in a while a partridge is born of unusual size and vigor, whose ruff is not only larger, but by a peculiar kind of intensification is of a deep coppery red, iridescent with violet, green, and gold. Such a bird is sure to be a wonder to all who know him, and the little one who had squatted on the chip, and had always done what he was told, developed before the Acorn Moon had changed, into all the glory of a gold and copper ruff—for this was Redruff, the famous partridge of the Don Valley.

IV

One day late in the Acorn Moon, that is, about mid-October, as the grouse family were basking with full crops near a great pine log on the sunlit edge of the beaver-meadow, they heard the far-away bang of a gun, and Redruff, acting on some impulse from within, leaped on the log, strutted up and down a couple of times, then, yielding to the elation of the bright, clear, bracing air, he whirred his wings in loud defiance. Then, giving fuller vent to this expression of vigor, just as a colt frisks to show how well he feels, he whirred yet more loudly, until, unwittingly, he found himself drumming, and tickled with the discovery of his new power, thumped the air again and again till he filled the near woods with the loud tattoo of the fully grown cock-partridge. His brother and sister heard and looked on with admiration and surprise; so did his mother, but from that time she began to be a little afraid of him.

In early November comes the moon of a weird foe. By a strange law of nature, not wholly without parallel among mankind, all partridges go crazy in the November moon of their first year. They become possessed of a mad hankering to get away somewhere, it does not matter much where. And the wisest of them do all sorts of foolish things at this period. They go drifting, perhaps, at speed over the country by night, and are cut in two by wires, or dash into lighthouses, or locomotive head-lights. Daylight finds them in all sorts of absurd places, in buildings, in open marshes, perched on telephone wires in a great city, or even on board of coasting vessels. The craze seems to be a relic of a bygone habit of migra-tion, and it has at least one good effect, it breaks up the families and prevents the constant intermarrying, which would surely be fatal to their race. It always takes the young badly their first year, and they may have it again the second fall, for it is very catching; but in the third season it is practically unknown.

Redruff's mother knew it was coming as soon as she saw the frost grapes blackening, and the maples shedding their crimson and gold. There was nothing to do but care for their health and keep them in the quietest part of the woods.

The first sign of it came when a flock of wild geese went *honking* southward overhead. The young ones had never before seen such long-necked hawks, and were afraid of them. But seeing that their mother had no fear, they took courage, and watched them with intense interest. Was it the wild, clanging cry that moved them, or was it solely the inner prompting then come to the surface? A strange longing to follow took possession of each of the young ones. They watched those arrowy trumpeters fading away to the south, and sought out higher perches to watch them farther yet, and from that time things were no n.ore the same. The November moon was waxing, and when it was full, the November madness came.

The least vigorous of the flock were most affected. The little family was scattered. Redruff himself flew on several long erratic night journeys. The impulse took him southward, but there lay the boundless stretch of Lake Ontario, so he turned again, and the waning of the Mad Moon found him once more in the Mud Creek Glen, but absolutely alone.

V

Food grew scarce as winter wore on. Redruff clung to the old ravine and the piney sides of Taylor's Hill, but every month brought its food and its foes. The Mad Moon brought madness, solitude, and grapes; the Snow Moon came with rosehips; and the Stormy Moon brought browse of birch and silver storms that sheathed the woods in ice, and made it hard to keep one's perch while pulling off the frozen buds. Redruff's beak grew terribly worn with the work, so that even when closed there was still an opening through behind the hook. But nature had prepared him for the slippery footing; his toes, so slim and trim in September, had sprouted rows of sharp, horny points, and these grew with the growing cold, till the first snow had found him fully equipped with snow-shoes and ice-creepers. The cold weather had driven away most of the hawks and owls, and made it impossible for his four-footed enemies to approach unseen, so that things were nearly balanced.

His flight in search of food had daily led him

farther on, till he had discovered and explored the Rosedale Creek, with its banks of silver-birch, and Castle Frank, with its grapes and rowan berries, as well as Chester woods, where amelanchier and Virginia-creeper swung their fruit-bunches, and checkerberries glowed beneath the snow.

He soon found out that for some strange reason men with guns did not go within the high fence of Castle Frank. So among these scenes he lived his life, learning new places, new foods, and grew wiser and more beautiful every day.

He was quite alone so far as kindred were concerned, but that scarcely seemed a hardship. Wherever he went he could see the jolly chickadees scrambling merrily about, and he remembered the time when they had seemed such big, important creatures. They were the most absurdly cheerful things in the woods. Before the autumn was fairly over they had begun to sing their famous refrain, '*Spring Soon*,' and kept it up with good heart more or less all through the winter's direst storms, till at length the waning of the Hungry Moon, our February, seemed really to lend some point to the ditty, and they redoubled their optimistic announcement to the world in an 'I-told-you-so' mood.

Soon good support was found, for the sun gained strength and melted the snow from the southern slope of Castle Frank Hill, and exposed great banks of fragrant wintergreen, whose berries were a bounteous feast for Redruff, and, ending the hard work of pulling frozen browse, gave his bill the needed chance to grow into its proper shape again. Very soon the first bluebird came flying over and warbled as he flew ' *The spring is coming.*' The sun kept gaining, and early one day in the dark of the Wakening Moon of March there was a loud ' *Caw, caw*,' and old Silverspot, the king-crow, came swinging along from the south at the head of his troops and officially announced

' THE SPRING HAS COME.'

All nature seemed to respond to this, the opening of the birds' New Year, and yet it was something within that chiefly seemed to move them. The chickadees went simply wild; they sang their ' *Spring now, spring now now—Spring now now*,' so persistently that one wondered how they found time to get a living.

And Redruff felt it thrill him through and through. He sprang with joyous vigor on a stump and sent rolling down the little valley, again and again, a thundering ' *Thump, thump, thump, thunderrrrrrrr,*' that wakened dull echoes as it rolled, and voiced his gladness in the coming of the spring.

Away down the valley was Cuddy's shanty. He heard the drum-call on the still morning air and 'reckoned there was a cock patridge to git,' and came sneaking up the ravine with his gun. But Redruff skimmed away in silence, nor rested till once more in Mud Creek Glen. And there he mounted the very log where first he had drummed and rolled his loud tattoo again and again, till a small boy who had taken a short cut to the mill through the woods, ran home, badly scared, to tell his mother he was sure the Indians were on the war-path, for he heard their war-drums beating in the glen.

Why does a happy boy holla? Why does a lonesome youth sigh? They don't know any more than Redruff knew why every day now he mounted some dead log and thumped and thundered to the woods; then strutted and admired his gorgeous blazing ruffs as they flashed their jewels in the sunlight, and then thundered out again. Whence now came the strange wish for someone else to admire the plumes? And why had such a notion never come till the Pussywillow Moon?

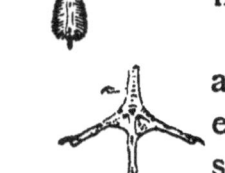

' *Thump, thump, thunder-r-r-r-r-r-rrrr* '
' *Thump, thump, thunder-r-r-r-r-r-rrrr* '
he rumbled again and again.

Day after day he sought the favorite log, and a new beauty, a rose-red comb, grew out above each clear, keen eye, and the clumsy snow-shoes were wholly shed from his feet. His ruff grew finer, his eye brighter, and his whole appearance splendid to behold, as he strutted and flashed in the sun. But—oh! he was *so lonesome now.*

Yet what could he do but blindly vent his hankering in this daily drum-parade, till on a day early in loveliest May, when the trilliums had fringed his log with silver stars, and he had drummed and longed, then drummed again, his keen ear caught a sound, a gentle footfall in the brush. He turned to a statue and watched; he knew he had been watched. Could it be possible? Yes! there it was—a form—another —a shy little lady grouse, now bashfully seeking to hide. In a moment he was by her side. His whole nature swamped by a new feeling— burnt up with thirst—a cooling spring in sight. And how he spread and flashed his proud array! How came he to know that that would please? He puffed his plumes and contrived to stand just right to catch the sun, and strutted and uttered a low, soft chuckle that must have been just as good as the 'sweet nothings' of another race, for clearly now her heart was won. Won, really, days ago, if only he had known. For full three days she had come at the loud tattoo and coyly admired him from afar, and felt a little piqued that he had not yet found her out, so close at hand. So it was not quite all mischance, perhaps, that that little stamp had caught his ear. But now she meekly bowed her head with sweet, submissive grace—the desert passed, the parch-burnt wanderer found the spring at last.

Oh, those were bright, glad days in the lovely glen of the unlovely name. The sun was never so bright, and the piney air was balmier sweet than dreams. And that great noble bird came daily on his log, sometimes with her and sometimes quite alone, and drummed for very joy of being alive. But why sometimes alone? Why not forever with his Brownie bride? Why should she stay to feast and play with him for hours, then take some stealthy chance to slip away and see him no more for hours or till next day, when his martial music from the log announced him restless for her quick return? There was a woodland mystery here he could not clear. Why should her stay with him grow daily less till it was down to minutes, and one day at last she never came at all.   Nor the next, nor the next, and Redruff, wild, careered on lightning wing and drummed on the old log, then away up-stream on another log, and skimmed the hill to another ravine to drum and drum.   But on the fourth day, when he came and loudly called her, as of old, at their earliest tryst, he heard a sound in the bushes, as at first, and there was his missing Brownie bride with ten little peep-ing partridges following after.

Redruff skimmed to her side, terribly fright-ening the bright-eyed downlings, and was just a little dashed to find the brood with claims far stronger than his own.   But he soon ac-cepted the change, and thenceforth joined him-self to the brood, caring for them as his father never had for him.

VI

Good fathers are rare in the grouse world. The mother-grouse builds her nest and hatch-es out her young without help.   She even hides the place of the nest from the father and meets him only at the drum-log and the feed-ing - ground, or perhaps the dusting - place, which is the club-house of the grouse kind.

When Brownie's little ones came out they had filled her every thought, even to the forgetting of their splendid father. But on the third day, when they were strong enough, she had taken them with her at the father's call.

Some fathers take no interest in their little ones, but Redruff joined at once to help Brownie in the task of rearing the brood. They had learned to eat and drink just as their father had learned long ago, and could toddle along, with their mother leading the way, while the father ranged near by or followed far behind.

The very next day, as they went from the hill-side down toward the creek in a somewhat drawn-out string, like beads with a big one at each end, a red squirrel, peeping around a pine-trunk, watched the processing of downlings with the Runtie straggling far in the rear. Redruff, yards behind, preening his feathers on a high log, had escaped the eye of the squirrel, whose strange, perverted thirst for birdling blood was roused at what seemed so fair a chance. With murderous intent to cut off the hindmost straggler, he made a dash. Brownie could not have seen him until too late, but Redruff did. He flew for that red-haired cutthroat; his weapons were his fists, that is, the knob-joints of the wings, and what a blow he could strike! At the first onset he struck the squirrel square on the end of the nose, his weakest spot, and sent him reeling; he staggered and wriggled into a brush-pile, where he had expected to carry the little grouse, and there lay gasping with red drops trickling down his wicked snout. The partridges left him lying there, and what became of him they never knew, but he troubled them no more.

The family went on toward the water, but a cow had left deep tracks in the sandy loam, and into one of these fell one of the chicks and peeped in dire distress when he found he could not get out.

This was a fix. Neither old one seemed to know what to do, but as they trampled vainly round the edge, the sandy bank caved in, and, running down, formed a long slope, up which the young one ran and rejoined his brothers under the broad veranda of their mother's tail.

Brownie was a bright little mother, of small stature, but keen of wit and sense, and was, night and day, alert to care for her darling chicks. How proudly she stepped and clucked through the arching woods with her dainty brood behind her; how she strained her little brown tail almost to a half-circle to give them

Redruff saving Runtie

a broader shade, and never flinched at sight of any foe, but held ready to fight or fly, whichever seemed the best for her little ones.

Before the chicks could fly they had a meeting with old Cuddy; though it was June, he was out with his gun. Up the third ravine he went, and Tike, his dog, ranging ahead, came so dangerously near the Brownie brood that Redruff ran to meet him, and by the old but never-failing trick led him on a foolish chase away back down the valley of the Don.

But Cuddy, as it chanced, came right along, straight for the brood, and Brownie, giving the signal to the children, '*Krrr, krrr*' (Hide, hide), ran to lead the man away just as her mate had led the dog. Full of a mother's devoted love, and skilled in the learning of the woods she ran in silence till quite near, then sprang with a roar of wings right in his face, and tumbling on the leaves she shammed a lameness that for a moment deceived the poacher. But when she dragged one wing and whined about his feet, then slowly crawled away, he knew just what it meant—that it was all a trick to lead him from her brood, and he struck at her a savage blow; but little Brownie was quick, she avoided the blow and limped behind a sapling, there to beat herself upon

the leaves again in sore distress, and seem so
lame that Cuddy made another try to strike
her down with a stick. But she moved in
time to balk him, and bravely, steadfast still to
lead him from her helpless little ones, she flung
herself before him and beat her gentle breast
upon the ground and moaned as though begging for mercy. And Cuddy, failing again to
strike her, raised his gun, and firing charge
enough to kill a bear, he blew poor brave, devoted Brownie into quivering, bloody rags.

This gunner brute knew the young must be
hiding near, so looked about to find them. But
no one moved or peeped. He saw not one, but
as he tramped about with heedless, hateful feet,
he crossed and crossed again their hiding-
ground, and more than one of the silent little
sufferers he trampled to death, and neither
knew nor cared.

Redruff had taken the yellow brute away off
down-stream, and now returned to where he
left his mate. The murderer had gone, taking
her remains, to be thrown to the dog. Redruff
sought about and found the bloody spot with
feathers, Brownie's feathers, scattered around,
and now he knew the meaning of that shot.

Who can tell what his horror and his mourn-
ing were? The outward signs were few, some

minutes dumbly gazing at the place with down-
cast, draggled look, and then a change at the
thought of their helpless brood. Back to the
hiding-place he went, and called the well-known
'*Kreet, kreet.*' Did every grave give up its little inmate at the magic word? No, barely
more than half; six little balls of down un-
veiled their lustrous eyes, and, rising, ran to
meet him, but four feathered little bodies had
found their graves indeed. Redruff called
again and again, till he was sure that all who
could respond had come, then led them from
that dreadful place, far, far away up-stream,
where barbed-wire fences and bramble thickets
were found to offer a less grateful, but more reliable, shelter.

Here the brood grew and were trained by
their father just as his mother had trained him;
though wider knowledge and experience gave
him many advantages. He knew so well the
country round and all the feeding-grounds, and
how to meet the ills that harass partridge-life,
that the summer passed and not a chick was
lost. They grew and flourished, and when the
Gunner Moon arrived they were a fine family
of six grown-up grouse with Redruff, splendid
in his gleaming copper feathers, at their head.
He had ceased to drum during the summer

after the loss of Brownie, but drumming is to the partridge what singing is to the lark; while it is his love-song, it is also an expression of exuberance born of health, and when the molt was over and September food and weather had renewed his splendid plumes and braced him up again, his spirits revived, and finding himself one day near the old log he mounted impulsively, and drummed again and again.

From that time he often drummed, while his children sat around, or one who showed his father's blood would mount some nearby stump or stone, and beat the air in the loud tattoo.

The black grapes and the Mad Moon now came on. But Redruff's brood were of a vigorous stock; their robust health meant robust wits, and though they got the craze, it passed within a week, and only three had flown away for good.

Redruff, with his remaining three, was living in the glen when the snow came. It was light, flaky snow, and as the weather was not very cold, the family squatted for the night under the low, flat boughs of a cedar-tree. But next day the storm continued, it grew colder, and the drifts piled up all day. At night the snowfall ceased, but the frost grew harder still, so Redruff, leading the family to a birch-tree above a deep drift, dived into the snow, and the others did the same. Then into the holes the wind blew the loose snow—their pure white bed-clothes, and thus tucked in they slept in com-fort, for the snow is a warm wrap, and the air passes through it easily enough for breathing. Next morning each partridge found a solid wall of ice before him from his frozen breath, but easily turned to one side and rose on the wing at Redruff's morning '*Kreet, kreet, kwit.*' (Come children, come children, fly.)

This was the first night for them in a snow-drift, though it was an old story to Redruff, and next night they merrily dived again into bed, and the north wind tucked them in as before. But a change of weather was brewing. The night wind veered to the east. A fall of heavy flakes gave place to sleet, and that to silver rain. The whole wide world was sheathed in ice, and when the grouse awoke to quit their beds, they found themselves sealed in with a great, cruel sheet of edgeless ice.

The deeper snow was still quite soft, and Redruff bored his way to the top, but there the hard, white sheet defied his strength. Hammer and struggle as he might he could make no im-pression, and only bruised his wings and head. His life had been made up of keen joys and dull hardships, with frequent sudden desperate straits, but this seemed the hardest brunt of all, as the slow hours wore on and found him weakening with his struggles, but no nearer to freedom. He could hear the struggling of his family, too, or sometimes heard them calling to him for help with their long-drawn plaintive '*p-c-c-c-c-e-t-e, p-c-c-e-e-e-t-c.*'

They were hidden from many of their enemies, but not from the pangs of hunger, and when the night came down the weary prisoners, worn out with hunger and useless toil, grew quiet in despair. At first they had been afraid the fox would come and find them imprisoned there at his mercy, but as the second night went slowly by they no longer cared, and even wished he would come and break the crusted snow, and so give them at least a fighting chance for life.

But when the fox really did come padding over the frozen drift, the deep-laid love of life revived, and they crouched in utter stillness till he passed. The second day was one of driving storm. The north wind sent his snowhorses, hissing and careering over the white earth, tossing and curling their white manes and kicking up more snow as they dashed on. The long, hard grinding of the granular snow seemed to be thinning the snow-crust, for though far from dark below, it kept on growing lighter. Redruff had pecked and pecked at the under side all day, till his head ached and his bill was wearing blunt, but when the sun went down he seemed as far as ever from escape. The night passed like the others, except no fox went trotting overhead. In the morning he renewed his pecking, though now with scarcely any force, and the voices or struggles of the others were no more heard. As the daylight grew stronger he could see that his long efforts had made a brighter spot above him in the snow, and he continued feebly pecking. Outside, the storm-horses kept on trampling all day, the crust was really growing thin under their heels, and late that afternoon his bill went through into the open air. New life came with this gain, and he pecked away, till just before the sun went down he had made a hole that his head, his neck, and his ever-beautiful ruffs could pass. His great, broad shoulders were too large, but he could now strike downward, which gave him fourfold force; the snow-crust crumbled quickly, and in a little while he sprang from his icy prison once more free. But the young ones! Redruff flew to the nearest bank, hastily gathered a few red

hips to stay his gnawing hunger, then returned to the prison-drift and clucked and
stamped. He got only one reply, a feeble
'*peete, peete,*' and scratching with his sharp
claws on the thinned granular sheet he soon
broke through, and Graytail feebly crawled out
of the hole. But that was all; the others, scattered he could not tell where in the drift, made
no reply, gave no sign of life, and he was forced
to leave them. When the snow melted in the
spring their bodies came to view, skin, bones,
and feathers—nothing more.

VII

It was long before Redruff and Graytail fully
recovered, but food and rest in plenty are sure
cure-alls, and a bright, clear day in midwinter
had the usual effect of setting the vigorous
Redruff to drumming on the log. Was it the
drumming, or the tell-tale tracks of their snow-
shoes on the omnipresent snow, that betrayed
them to Cuddy? He came prowling again and
again up the ravine, with dog and gun, intent
to hunt the partridges down. They knew him
of old, and he was coming now to know them
well. That great copper-ruffed cock was be-
coming famous up and down the valley. Dur-

ing the Gunner Moon many a one had tried to
end his splendid life, just as a worthless wretch
of old sought fame by burning the Ephesian
wonder of the world. But Redruff was deep
in woodcraft. He knew just where to hide,
and when to rise on silent wing, and when to
squat till overstepped, then rise on thunder
wing within a yard to shield himself at once
behind some mighty tree-trunk and speed
away.

But Cuddy never ceased to follow with his
gun that red-ruffed cock; many a long snap-
shot he tried, but somehow always found a tree,
a bank, or some safe shield between, and Redruff lived and throve and drummed.

When the Snow Moon came he moved with
Graytail to the Castle Frank woods, where
food was plenty as well as grand old trees.
There was in particular, on the east slope
among the creeping hemlocks, a splendid pine.
It was six feet through, and its first branches
began at the tops of the other trees. Its top
in summer-time was a famous resort for the
bluejay and his bride. Here, far beyond the
reach of shot, in warm spring days the jay
would sing and dance before his mate, spread
his bright blue plumes and warble the sweetest
fairyland music, so sweet and soft that few hear

it but the one for whom it is meant, and books know nothing at all about it.

This great pine had an especial interest for Redruff, now living near with his remaining young one, but its base, not its far-away crown, concerned him. All around were low, creeping hemlocks, and among them the partridge-vine and the wintergreen grew, and the sweet black acorns could be scratched from under the snow. There was no better feeding-ground, for when that insatiable gunner came on them there it was easy to run low among the hemlock to the great pine, then rise with a derisive *whirr* behind its bulk, and keeping the huge trunk in line with the deadly gun, skim off in safety. A dozen times at least the pine had saved them during the lawful murder season, and here it was that Cuddy, knowing their feeding habits, laid a new trap. Under the bank he sneaked and watched in ambush while an accomplice went around the Sugar Loaf to drive the birds. He came trampling through the low thicket where Redruff and Graytail were feeding, and long before the gunner was dangerously near Redruff gave a low warning '*rrr-rrr*' (danger) and walked quickly toward the great pine in case they had to rise.

Graytail was some distance up the hill, and

suddenly caught sight of a new foe close at hand, the yellow cur, coming right on. Redruff, much farther off, could not see him for the bushes, and Graytail became greatly alarmed.

'*Kwit, kwit*' (Fly, fly), she cried, running down the hill for a start. '*Kreet, k-r-r-r*' (This way, hide), cried the cooler Redruff, for he saw that now the man with the gun was getting in range. He gained the great trunk, and behind it, as he paused a moment to call earnestly to Graytail, 'This way, this way,' he heard a slight noise under the bank before him that betrayed the ambush, then there was a terrified cry from Graytail as the dog sprang at her, she rose in air and skimmed behind the shielding trunk, away from the gunner in the open, right into the power of the miserable wretch under the bank.

Whirr, and up she went, a beautiful, sentient, noble being.

Bang, and down she fell—battered and bleeding, to gasp her life out and to lie a rumpled mass of carrion in the snow.

It was a perilous place for Redruff. There was no chance for a safe rise, so he squatted low. The dog came within ten feet of him, and the stranger, coming across to Cuddy, passed at five feet, but he never moved till a chance came to slip behind the great trunk away from both. Then he safely rose and flew to the lonely glen by Taylor's Hill.

One by one the deadly cruel gun had stricken his near ones down, till now, once more, he was alone. The Snow Moon slowly passed with many a narrow escape, and Redruff, now known to be the only survivor of his kind, was relentlessly pursued, and grew wilder every day.

It seemed, at length, a waste of time to follow him with a gun, so when the snow was deepest, and food scarcest, Cuddy hatched a new plot. Right across the feeding-ground, almost the only good one now in the Stormy Moon, he set a row of snares. A cottontail rabbit, an old friend, cut several of these with his sharp teeth, but some remained, and Redruff, watching a far-off   k that might turn out a hawk, trod right ir.   ... of them, and in an instant was jerked into the air to dangle by one foot.

Have the wild things no moral or legal rights? What right has man to inflict such long and fearful agony on a fellow-creature, simply because that creature does not speak his language? All that day, with growing, racking pains, poor Redruff hung and beat his great, strong wings in helpless struggles to be free. All day, all night, with growing torture, until he only longed for death. But no one came. The morning broke, the day wore on, and still he hung there, slowly dying ; his very strength a curse. The second night crawled slowly down, and when, in the dawdling hours of darkness, a great Horned Owl, drawn by the feeble flutter of a dying wing, cut short the pain, the deed was wholly kind.

The wind blew down the valley from the north. The snow-horses went racing over the wrinkled ice, over the Don Flats, and over the marsh toward the lake, white, for they were driven snow, but on them, scattered dark, were riding plumy fragments of partridge ruffs—the famous rainbow ruffs. And they rode on the wind that night, away, away to the south, over the dark lake, as they rode in the gloom of his Mad Moon flight, riding and riding on till they were engulfed, the last trace of the last of the Don Valley race.

For no partridge is heard in Castle Frank now—and in Mud Creek Ravine the old pine drum-log, unused, has rotted in silence away.

RAGGYLUG

THE STORY OF A COTTONTAIL RABBIT

RAGGYLUG

THE STORY OF A COTTONTAIL RABBIT

R AGGYLUG, or Rag, was the name of a
young cottontail rabbit.   It was given
him from his torn and ragged ear, a
life-mark that he got in his first adventure.
He lived with his mother in Olifant's swamp,
where I made their acquaintance and gathered,
in a hundred different ways, the little bits of
proof and scraps of truth that at length enabled
me to write this history.

Those who do not know the animals well
may think I have humanized them, but those
who have lived so near them as to know somewhat of their ways and their minds will not
think so.

Truly rabbits have no speech as we understand it, but they have a way of conveying
ideas by a system of sounds, signs, scents,
whisker-touches, movements, and example that
answers the purpose of speech ; and it must be

remembered that though in telling this story I freely translate from rabbit into English, *I repeat nothing that they did not say.*

I

The rank swamp grass bent over and concealed the snug nest where Raggylug's mother had hidden him. She had partly covered him with some of the bedding, and, as always, her last warning was to 'lay low and say nothing, whatever happens.' Though tucked in bed, he was wide awake and his bright eyes were taking in that part of his little green world that was straight above. A bluejay and a red-squirrel, two notorious thieves, were loudly berating each other for stealing, and at one time Rag's home bush was the centre of their fight; a yellow warbler caught a blue butterfly but six inches from his nose, and a scarlet and black ladybug, serenely waving her knobbed feelers, took a long walk up one grassblade, down another, and across the nest and over Rag's face —and yet he never moved nor even winked.

After awhile he heard a strange rustling of the leaves in the near thicket. It was an odd, continuous sound, and though it went this way and that way and came ever nearer, there was

"Mammy, Mammy!" he screamed, in mortal terror.

no patter of feet with it. Rag had lived his whole life in the swamp (he was three weeks old) and yet had never heard anything like this. Of course his curiosity was greatly aroused. His mother had cautioned him to lay low, but that was understood to be in case of danger, and this strange sound without footfalls could not be any to fear.

The low rasping went past close at hand, then to the right, then back, and seemed going away. Rag felt he knew what he was about ; he wasn't a baby; it was his duty to learn what it was. He slowly raised his roly-poly body on his short, fluffy legs, lifted his little round head above the covering of his nest and peeped out into the woods. The sound had ceased as soon as he moved. He saw nothing, so took one step forward to a clear view, and instantly found himself face to face with an enormous Black Serpent.

" Mammy," he screamed in mortal terror as the monster darted at him. With all the strength of his tiny limbs he tried to run. But in a flash the Snake had him by one ear and whipped around him with his coils to gloat over the helpless little baby bunny he had secured for dinner.

" Mam-my — Mam-my," gasped poor little

Raggylug as the cruel monster began slowly choking him to death. Very soon the little one's cry would have ceased, but bounding through the woods straight as an arrow came Mammy. No longer a shy, helpless little Molly Cottontail, ready to fly from a shadow: the mother's love was strong in her. The cry of her baby had filled her with the courage of a hero, and—hop, she went over that horrible reptile. Whack, she struck down at him with her sharp hind claws as she passed, giving him such a stinging blow that he squirmed with pain and hissed with anger.

" M-a-m-m-y," came feebly from the little one. And Mammy came leaping again and again and struck harder and fiercer until the loathsome reptile let go the little one's ear and tried to bite the old one as she leaped over. But all he got was a mouthful of wool each time, and Molly's fierce blows began to tell, as long bloody rips were torn in the Black Snake's scaly armor.

Things were now looking bad for the Snake ; and bracing himself for the next charge, he lost his tight hold on Baby Bunny, who at once wriggled out of the coils and away into the underbrush, breathless and terribly fright- ened, but unhurt save that his left ear was

much torn by the teeth of that dreadful Serpent.

Molly had now gained all she wanted. She
had no notion of fighting for glory or revenge.
Away she went into the woods and the little
one followed the shining beacon of her snow-
white tail until she led him to a safe corner of
the Swamp.

II

Old Olifant's Swamp was a rough, brambly
tract of second-growth woods, with a marshy
pond and a stream through the middle. A
few ragged remnants of the old forest still
stood in it and a few of the still older trunks
were lying about as dead logs in the brush-
wood. The land about the pond was of that
willow-grown, sedgy kind that cats and horses
avoid, but that cattle do not fear. The drier
zones were overgrown with briars and young
trees. The outermost belt of all, that next the
fields, was of thrifty, gummy-trunked young
pines whose living needles in air and dead
ones on earth offer so delicious an odor to the
nostrils of the passer - by, and so deadly a
breath to those seedlings that would compete
with them for the worthless waste they grow
on.

All around for a long way were smooth fields, and the only wild tracks that ever crossed these fields were those of a thoroughly bad and unscrupulous fox that lived only too near.

The chief indwellers of the swamp were Molly and Rag. Their nearest neighbors were far away, and their nearest kin were dead. This was their home, and here they lived together, and here Rag received the training that made his success in life.

Molly was a good little mother and gave him a careful bringing up. The first thing he learned was 'to lay low and say nothing.' His adventure with the snake taught him the wisdom of this. Rag never forgot that lesson; afterward he did as he was told, and it made the other things come more easily.

The second lesson he learned was 'freeze.' It grows out of the first, and Rag was taught it as soon as he could run.

'Freezing' is simply doing nothing, turning into a statue. As soon as he finds a foe near, no matter what he is doing, a well-trained Cottontail keeps just as he is and stops all movement, for the creatures of the woods are of the same color as the things in the woods and catch the eye only while moving. So when enemies chance together, the one who first sees the other can keep himself unseen by 'freezing' and thus have all the advantage of choosing the time for attack or escape. Only those who live in the woods know the importance of this; every wild creature and every hunter must learn it; all learn to do it well, but not one of them can beat Molly Cottontail in the doing. Rag's mother taught him this trick by example. When the white cotton cushion that she always carried to sit on went bobbing away through the woods, of course Rag ran his hardest to keep up. But when Molly stopped and 'froze,' the natural wish to copy made him do the same.

But the best lesson of all that Rag learned from his mother was the secret of the Brier-brush. It is a very old secret now, and to make it plain you must first hear why the Brierbrush quarrelled with the beasts.

Long ago the Roses used to grow on bushes that had no thorns. But the Squirrels and Mice used to climb after them, the cattle used to knock them off with their horns, the Possum would twitch them off with his long tail, and the Deer, with his sharp hoofs, would break them down. So the Brierbrush armed itself with spikes to protect its roses and declared eternal war on all creat-

ures that climbed trees, or had horns, or hoofs, or long tails. This left the Brierbrush at peace with none but Molly Cottontail, who could not climb, was hornless, hoofless and had scarcely any tail at all.

In truth the Cottontail had never harmed a Brierrose, and having now so many enemies the Rose took the Rabbit into especial friendship, and when dangers are threatening poor Bunny he flies to the nearest Brierbrush, certain that it is ready, with a million keen and poisoned daggers, to defend him.

So the secret that Rag learned from his mother was, ' The Brierbrush is your best friend.'

Much of the time that season was spent in learning the lay of the land, and the bramble and brier mazes. And Rag learned them so well that he could go all around the swamp by two different ways and never leave the friendly briers at any place for more than five hops.

It is not long since the foes of the Cottontails were disgusted to find that man had brought a new kind of bramble and planted it in long lines throughout the country. It was so strong that no creatures could break it down, and so sharp that the toughest skin was torn by it. Each year there was more of it and each year it became a more serious matter to the wild creatures. But Molly Cottontail had no fear of it. She was not brought up in the briers for nothing. Dogs and foxes, cattle and sheep, and even man himself might be torn by those fearful spikes : but Molly understands it and lives and thrives under it. And the further it spreads the more safe country there is for the Cottontail. And the name of this new and dreaded bramble is—*the barbed-wire fence.*

III

Molly had no other children to look after now, so Rag had all her care. He was unusually quick and bright as well as strong, and he had uncommonly good chances; so he got on remarkably well.

All the season she kept him busy learning the tricks of the trail, and what to eat and drink and what not to touch. Day by day she worked to train him; little by little she taught him, putting into his mind hundreds of ideas that her own life or early training had stored in hers, and so equipped him with the knowledge that makes life possible to their kind.

Close by her side in the clover-field or the thicket he would sit and copy her when she wobbled her nose ' to keep her smeller clear,' and pull the bite from her mouth or taste her lips to make sure he was getting the same kind of fodder. Still copying her, he learned to comb his ears with his claws and to dress his coat and to bite the burrs out of his vest and socks. He learned, too, that nothing but clear dewdrops from the briers were fit for a rabbit to drink, as water which has once touched the earth must surely bear some taint. Thus he began the study of woodcraft, the oldest of all sciences.

As soon as Rag was big enough to go out alone, his mother taught him the signal code. Rabbits telegraph each other by thumping on the ground with their hind feet. Along the ground sound carries far ; a thump that at six feet from the earth is not heard at twenty yards will, near the ground, be heard at least one hundred yards. Rabbits have very keen hearing, and so might hear this same thump at two hundred yards, and that would reach from end to end of Olifant's Swamp. A single *thump* means 'look out' or 'freeze.' A slow *thump thump* means 'come.' A fast *thump thump* means 'danger ;' and a very fast *thump thump thump* means 'run for dear life.'

At another time, when the weather was fine and the bluejays were quarrelling among themselves, a sure sign that no dangerous foe was about, Rag began a new study. Molly, by flattening her ears, gave the sign to squat. Then she ran far away in the thicket and gave the thumping signal for 'come.' Rag set out at a run to the place but could not find Molly. He thumped, but got no reply. Setting carefully about his search he found her foot-scent, and following this strange guide, that the beasts all know so well and man does not know at all, he worked out the trail and found her where she was hidden. Thus he got his first lesson in trailing, and thus it was that the games of hide and seek they played became the schooling for the serious chase of which there was so much in his after-life.

Before that first season of schooling was over he had learnt all the principal tricks by which a rabbit lives, and in not a few problems showed himself a veritable genius.

He was an adept at 'tree,' 'dodge,' and 'squat;' he could play 'log-lump' with 'wind,' and 'baulk' with 'back-track' so well that he scarcely needed any other tricks. He had not yet tried it, but he knew just how to play 'barb-wire,' which is a new trick of the brilliant order; he had made a special study of 'sand,' which burns up all scent, and he was

deeply versed in 'change-off,' 'fence,'. and
'double,' as well as 'hole-up,' which is a trick
requiring longer notice, and yet he never forgot that 'lay-low' is the beginning of all wisdom and 'brierbrush' the only trick that is
always safe.

He was taught the signs by which to know
all his foes and then the way to baffle them.
For hawks, owls, foxes, hounds, curs, minks,
weasels, cats, skunks, coons, and men, each
have a different plan of pursuit, and for
each and all of these evils he was taught
a remedy.

And for knowledge of the enemy's approach
he learnt to depend first on himself and his
mother, and then on the bluejay. "Never neg-
lect the bluejay's warning," said Molly; " he is
a mischief-maker, a marplot, and a thief all the
time, but ncthing escapes him. He wouldn't
mind harming us, but he cannot, thanks to the
briers, and his enemies are ours, so it is well to
heed him. If the woodpecker cries a warning
you can trust him, he is honest; but he is a fool
beside the bluejay, and though the bluejay often tells lies for mischief you are safe to believe
him when he brings ill news."

The barbed-wire trick takes a deal of nerve
and the best of legs. It was long before Rag

ventured to play it, but as he came to his full powers it became one of his favorites.

"It's fine play for those who can do it," said Molly. "First you lead off your dog on a straightaway and warm him up a bit by nearly letting him catch you. Then keeping just one hop ahead, you lead him at a long slant full tilt into a breast-high barb-wire. I've seen many a dog and fox crippled, and one big hound killed outright this way. But I've also seen more than one rabbit lose his life in trying it."

Rag early learnt what some rabbits never learn at all, that 'hole-up' is not such a fine ruse as it seems; it may be the certain safety of a wise rabbit, but soon or late is a sure death-trap to a fool. A young rabbit always thinks of it first, an old rabbit never tries it till all others fail. It means escape from a man or dog, a fox or a bird of prey, but it means sudden death if the foe is a ferret, mink, skunk, or weasel.

There were but two ground-holes in the Swamp. One on the Sunning Bank, which was a dry sheltered knoll in the South-end. It was open and sloping to the sun, and here on fine days the Cottontails took their sunbaths. They stretched out among the fragrant pine needles and winter-green in odd, cat-like positions, and turned slowly over as though roasting and wishing all sides well done. And they blinked and panted, and squirmed as if in dreadful pain; yet this was one of the keenest enjoyments they knew.

Just over the brow of the knoll was a large pine stump. Its grotesque roots wriggled out above the yellow sand-bank like dragons, and under their protecting claws a sulky old woodchuck had digged a den long ago. He became more sour and ill-tempered as weeks went by, and one day waited to quarrel with Olifant's dog instead of going in, so that Molly Cottontail was able to take possession of the den an hour later.

This, the pine-root hole, was afterward very coolly taken by a self-sufficient young skunk, who with less valor might have enjoyed greater longevity, for he imagined that even man with a gun would fly from him. Instead of keeping Molly from the den for good, therefore, his reign, like that of a certain Hebrew king, was over in four days.

The other, the fern-hole, was in a fern thicket next the clover field. It was small and damp, and useless except as a last retreat. It also was the work of a woodchuck, a well-meaning, friendly neighbor, but a hare-brained youngster whose skin in the form of a whip-lash was now developing higher horse-power in the Olifant working team.

"Simple justice," said the old man, "for that hide was raised on stolen feed that the team would 'a' turned into horse-power anyway."

The Cottontails were now sole owners of the holes, and did not go near them when they could help it, lest anything like a path should be made that might betray these last retreats to an enemy.

There was also the hollow hickory, which, though nearly fallen, was still green, and had the great advantage of being open at both ends. This had long been the residence of one Lotor, a solitary old coon whose ostensible calling was frog-hunting, and who, like the monks of old, was supposed to abstain from all flesh food. But it was shrewdly suspected that he needed but a chance to indulge in a diet of rabbit. When at last one dark night he was killed while raiding Olifant's hen-house, Molly, so far from feeling a pang of regret, took possession of his cosy nest with a sense of unbounded relief.

IV

Bright August sunlight was flooding the Swamp in the morning. Everything seemed soaking in the warm radiance. A little brown swamp-sparrow was teetering on a long rush in the pond. Beneath him there were open spaces of dirty water that brought down a few scraps of the blue sky, and worked it and the yellow duckweed into an exquisite mosaic, with a little wrong-side picture of the bird in the middle. On the bank behind was a great vigorous growth of golden green skunk-cabbage, that cast a dense shadow over the brown swamp tussocks.

The eyes of the swamp-sparrow were not trained to take in the color glories, but he saw what we might have missed; that two of the numberless leafy brown bumps under the broad cabbage-leaves were furry, living things, with noses that never ceased to move up and down whatever else was still.

It was Molly and Rag. They were stretched under the skunk-cabbage, not because they liked its rank smell, but because the winged ticks could not stand it at all and so left them in peace.

Rabbits have no set time for lessons, they are always learning ; but what the lesson is de-

pends on the present stress, and that must ar-
rive before it is known. They went to this
place for a quiet rest, but had not been long
there when suddenly a warning note from the
ever-watchful bluejay caused Molly's nose and
ears to go up and her tail to tighten to her
back. Away across the Swamp was Olifant's
big black and white dog, coming straight
toward them.

"Now," said Molly, "squat while I go and
keep that fool out of mischief." Away she
went to meet him and she fearlessly dashed
across the dog's path.

"Bow-ow-ow," he fairly yelled as he bounded
after Molly, but she kept just beyond his reach
and led him where the million daggers struck
fast and deep, till his tender ears were scratched
raw, and guided him at last plump into a hidden barbed-wire fence, where he got such a
gashing that he went homeward howling with
pain. After making a short double, a loop and
a baulk in case the dog should come back,
Molly returned to find that Rag in his eager-
ness was standing bolt upright and craning his
neck to see the sport.

This disobedience made her so angry that
she struck him with her hind foot and knocked
him over in the mud.

One day as they fed on the near clover field a red-tailed hawk came swooping after them. Molly kicked up her hind legs to make fun of him and skipped into the briers along one of their old pathways, where of course the hawk could not follow. It was the main path from the Creekside Thicket to the Stove-pipe brush-pile. Several creepers had grown across it, and Molly, keeping one eye on the hawk, set to work and cut the creepers off. Rag watched her, then ran on ahead, and cut some more that were across the path. "That's right," said Molly, "always keep the runways clear, you will need them often enough. Not wide, but clear. Cut everything like a creeper across them and some day you will find you have cut a snare. "A what?" asked Rag, as he scratched his right ear with his left hind foot.

"A snare is something that looks like a creeper, but it doesn't grow and it's worse than all the hawks in the world," said Molly, glancing at the now far-away red-tail, "for there it hides night and day in the runway till the chance to catch you comes."

"I don't believe it could catch me," said Rag, with the pride of youth as he rose on his heels to rub his chin and whiskers high up on a smooth sapling. Rag did not know he was doing this, but his mother saw and knew it was a sign, like the changing of a boy's voice, that her little one was no longer a baby but would soon be a grown-up Cottontail.

V

There is magic in running water. Who does not know it and feel it? The railroad builder fearlessly throws his bank across the wide bog or lake, or the sea itself, but the tiniest rill of running water he treats with great respect, studies its wish and its way and gives it all it seems to ask. The thirst-parched traveller in the poisonous alkali deserts holds back in deadly fear from the sedgy ponds till he finds one down whose centre is a thin, clear line, and a faint flow, the sign of running, living water, and joyfully he drinks.

There is magic in running water, no evil spell can cross it. Tam O'Shanter proved its potency in time of sorest need. The wild-wood creature with its deadly foe following tireless on the trail scent, realizes its nearing doom and feels an awful spell. Its strength is spent, its every trick is tried in vain till the good Angel leads it to the water, the running, living water, and dashing in it follows the cooling stream, and then with force renewed takes to the woods again.

There is magic in running water. The hounds come to the very spot and halt and cast about; and halt and cast in vain. Their spell is broken by the merry stream, and the wild thing lives its life.

And this was one of the great secrets that Raggylug learned from his mother—"after the Brierrose, the Water is your friend."

One hot, muggy night in August, Molly led Rag through the woods. The cotton-white cushion she wore under her tail twinkled ahead and was his guiding lantern, though it went out as soon as she stopped and sat on it. After a few runs and stops to listen, they came to the edge of the pond. The hylas in the trees above them were singing '*sleep, sleep,*' and away out on a sunken log in the deep water, up to his chin in the cooling bath, a bloated bullfrog was singing the praises of a '*jug o' rum.*'

" Follow me still," said Molly, in rabbit, and 'flop' she went into the pond and struck out for the sunken log in the middle. Rag flinched but plunged with a little 'ouch,' gasping and wobbling his nose very fast but still copying his mother. The same movements as on land sent him through the water, and thus he found he could swim. On he went till he reached the sunken log and scrambled up by his dripping mother on the high dry end, with a rushy screen around them and the Water that tells no tales. After this in warm, black nights, when that old fox from Springfield came prowling through the Swamp, Rag would note the place of the bullfrog's voice, for in case of direst need it might be a guide to safety. And thenceforth the words of the song that the bullfrog sang were, '*Come, come, in danger come.*'

This was the latest study that Rag took up with his mother—it was really a post-graduate course, for many little rabbits never learn it at all.

VI

No wild animal dies of old age. Its life has soon or late a tragic end. It is only a question of how long it can hold out against its foes. But Rag's life was proof that once a rabbit passes out of his youth he is likely to outlive his prime and be killed only in the last third of life, the downhill third we call old age.

The Cottontails had enemies on every side. Their daily life was a series of escapes. For dogs, foxes, cats, skunks, coons, weasels, minks, snakes, hawks, o vls, and men, and even insects were all plotting to kill them. They had hundreds of adventures, and at least once a day they had to fly for their lives and save themselves by their legs and wits.

More than once that hateful fox from Springfield drove them to taking refuge under the wreck of a barbed-wire hog-pen by the spring. But once there they could look calmly at him while he spiked his legs in vain attempts to reach them.

Once or twice Rag when hunted had played off the hound against a skunk that had seemed likely to be quite as dangerous as the dog.

Once he was caught alive by a hunter who had a hound and a ferret to help him. But Rag had the luck to escape next day, with a yet deeper distrust of ground holes. He was several times run into the water by the cat, and many times was chased by hawks and owls, bu for each kind of danger there was a safeguard. His mother taught him the principal dodges, and he improved on them and made many new ones as he grew older. And the older and wiser he grew the less he trusted to his legs, and the more to his wits for safety.

Ranger was the name of a young hound in the neighborhood. To train him his master used to put him on the trail of one of the Cottontails. It was nearly always Rag that they ran, for the young buck enjoyed the runs as much as they did, the spice of danger in them being just enough for zest. He would say :

" Oh, mother ! here comes the dog again, I must have a run to-day."

"You are too bold, Raggy, my son ! " she might reply. " I fear you will run once too often."

" But, mother, it is such glorious fun to tease that fool dog, and it's all good training. I'll thump if I am too hard pressed, then you can come and change off while I get my second wind."

On he would come, and Ranger would take the trail and follow till Rag got tired of it. Then he either sent a thumping telegram for help, which brought Molly to take charge of the dog, or he got rid of the dog by some clever trick. A description of one of these shows how well Rag had learned the arts of the woods.

He knew that his scent lay best near the ground, and was strongest when he was warm. So if he could get off the ground, and be left in peace for half an hour to cool off, and for the trail to stale, he knew he would be safe. When, therefore, he tired of the chase, he made for the Creekside brier-patch, where he ' wound '

—that .s, zigzagged—till he left a course so
crooked that the dog was sure to be greatly
delayed in working it out. He then went
straight to D in the woods, passing one hop to
windward of the high log E. Stopping at D, he
followed his back trail to F, here he leaped
aside and ran toward G. Then, returning on
his trail to J, he waited till the hound passed on
his trail at I. Rag then got back on his old

trail at H, and followed it to E, where, with a
scent-baulk or great leap aside, he reached the
high log, and running to its higher end, he sat
like a bump.

Ranger lost much time in the bramble maize,
and the scent was very poor when he got it
straightened out and came to D. Here he began
to circle to pick it up, and after losing much
time, struck the trail which ended suddenly at

G. Again he was at fault, and had to circle to find the trail. Wider and wider the circles, until at last, he passed right under the log Rag was on. But a cold scent, on a cold day, does not go downward much. Rag never budged nor winked, and the hound passed.

Again the dog came round. This time he crossed the low part of the log, and stopped to smell it. 'Yes, clearly it was rabbity,' but it was a stale scent now ; still he mounted the log.

It was a trying moment for Rag, as the great hound came sniff-sniffing along the log. But his nerve did not forsake him ; the wind was right ; he had his mind made up to bolt as soon as Ranger came half way up. But he didn't come. A yellow cur would have seen the rabbit sitting there, but the hound did not, and the scent seemed stale, so he leaped off the log, and Rag had won.

VII

Rag had never seen any other rabbit than his mother. Indeed he had scarcely thought about there being any other. He was more and more away from her now, and yet he never felt lonely, for rabbits do not hanker for company. But one day in December, while he was among the red dogwood brush, cutting a new path to the great Creekside thicket, he saw all at once against the sky over the Sunning Bank the head and ears of a strange rabbit. The new-comer had the air of a well-pleased discoverer and soon came hopping Rag's way along one of *his* paths into *his* Swamp. A new feeling rushed over him, that boiling mixture of anger and hatred called jealousy.

The stranger stopped at one of Rag's rubbing-trees—that is, a tree against which he used to stand on his ʾheels and rub his chin as far up as he could reach. He thought he did this simply because he liked it; but all buck-rabbits do so, and several ends are served. It makes the tree rabbity, so that other rabbits know that this swamp already belongs to a rabbit family and is not open for settlement. It also lets the next one know by the scent if the last caller was an acquaintance, and the height from the ground of the rubbing-places shows how tall the rabbit is.

Now to his disgust Rag noticed that the new-comer was a head taller than himself, and a big, stout buck at that. This was a wholly new experience and filled Rag with a wholly new feeling. The spirit of murder entered his heart;

he chewed very hard with nothing in his mouth, and hopping forward onto a smooth piece of hard ground he struck slowly:

' *Thump—thump—thump*,' which is a rabbit telegram for ' Get out of my swamp, or fight.'

The new-comer made a big V with his ears, sat upright for a few seconds, then, dropping on his fore-feet, sent along the ground a louder, stronger, ' *Thump—thump—thump.*'

And so war was declared.

They came together by short runs sidewise, each one trying to get the wind of the other and watching for a chance advantage. The stranger was a big, heavy buck with plenty of muscle, but one or two trifles such as treading on a turnover and failing to close when Rag was on low ground showed that he had not much cunning and counted on winning his battles by his weight. On he came at last and Rag met him like a little fury. As they came together they leaped up and struck out with their hind feet. *Thud, thud* they came, and down went poor little Rag. In a moment the stranger was on him with his teeth and Rag was bitten, and lost several tufts of hair before he could get up. But he was swift of foot and got out of reach. Again he charged and again he was knocked down and bitten severely.

He was no match for his foe, and it soon became a question of saving his own life.

Hurt as he was he sprang away, with the stranger in full chase, and bound to kill him as well as to oust him from the Swamp where he was born. Rag's legs were good and so was his wind. The stranger was big and so heavy that he soon gave up the chase, and it was well for poor Rag that he did, for he was getting stiff from his wounds as well as tired. From that day began a reign of terror for Rag. His training had been against owls, dogs, weasels, men, and so on, but what to do when chased by another rabbit, he did not know. All he knew was to lay low till he was found, then run.

Poor little Molly was completely terrorized; she could not help Rag and sought only to hide. But the big buck soon found her out. She tried to run from him, but she was not now so swift as Rag. The stranger made no attempt to kill her, but he made love to her, and because she hated him and tried to get away, he treated her shamefully. Day after day he worried her by following her about, and often, furious at her lasting hatred, he would knock her down and tear out mouthfuls of her soft fur till his rage cooled somewhat, when he would let her go for awhile. But his fixed purpose was to kill Rag, whose escape seemed hopeless. There was no other swamp he could go to, and whenever he took a nap now he had to be ready at any moment to dash for his life. A dozen times a day the big stranger came creeping up to where he slept, but each time the watchful Rag awoke in time to escape. To escape yet not to escape. He saved his life indeed, but oh! what a miserable life it had become. How maddening to be thus helpless, to see his little mother daily beaten and torn, as well as to see all his favorite feeding-grounds, the cosey nooks, and the pathways he had made with so much labor, forced from him by this hateful brute. Unhappy Rag realized that to the victor belong the spoils, and he hated him more than ever he did fox or ferret.

How was it to end? He was wearing out with running and watching and bad food, and little Molly's strength and spirit were breaking down under the long persecution. The stranger was ready to go to all lengths to destroy poor Rag, and at last stooped to the worst crime known among rabbits. However much they may hate each other, all good rabbits forget their feuds when their common

enemy appears. Yet one day when a great
goshawk came swooping over the Swamp, the
stranger, keeping well under cover himself,
tried again and again to drive Rag into the
open.

Once or twice the hawk nearly had him, but
still the briers saved him, and it was only when
the big buck himself came near being caught
that he gave it up. And again Rag escaped,
but was no better off. He made up his mind
to leave, with his mother, if possible, next night
and go into the world in quest of some new
home when he heard old Thunder, the hound,
sniffing and searching about the outskirts of
the swamp, and he resolved on playing a desperate game. He deliberately crossed the
hound's view, and the chase that then began
was fast and furious. Thrice around the
Swamp they went till Rag had made sure that
his mother was hidden safely and that his
hated foe was in his usual nest. Then right
into that nest and plump over him he jumped,
giving him a rap with one hind foot as he
passed over his head.

"You miserable fool, I kill you yet," cried
the stranger, and up he jumped only to find
himself between Rag and the dog and heir to
all the peril of the chase.

On came the hound baying hotly on the straight-away scent. The buck's weight and size were great advantages in a rabbit fight, but now they were fatal. He did not know many tricks. Just the simple ones like 'double,' 'wind,' and 'hole-up,' that every baby Bunny knows. But the chase was too close for doubling and winding, and he didn't know where the holes were.

It was a straight race. The brier-rose, kind to all rabbits alike, did its best, but it was no use. The baying of the hound was fast and steady. The crashing of the brush and the yelping of the hound each time the briers tore his tender ears were borne to the two rabbits where they crouched in hiding. But suddenly these sounds stopped, there was a scuffle, then loud and terrible screaming.

Rag knew what it meant and it sent a shiver through him, but he soon forgot that when all was over and rejoiced to be once more the master of the dear old Swamp.

VIII

Old Olifant had doubtless a right to burn all those brush-piles in the east and south of the

Swamp and to clear up the wreck of the old barbed-wire hog-pen just below the spring. But it was none the less hard on Rag and his mother. The first were their various residences and outposts, and the second their grand fastness and safe retreat.

They had so long held the Swamp and felt it to be their very own in every part and suburb —including Olifant's grounds and buildings— that they would have resented the appearance of another rabbit even about the adjoining barnyard.

Their claim, that of long, successful occupancy, was exactly the same as that by which most nations hold their land, and it would be hard to find a better right.

During the time of the January thaw the Olifants had cut the rest of the large wood about the pond and curtailed the Cottontails' domain on all sides. But they still clung to the dwindling Swamp, for it was their home and they were loath to move to foreign parts. Their life of daily perils went on, but they were still fleet of foot, long of wind, and bright of wit. Of late they had been somewhat troubled by a mink that had wandered up-stream to their quiet nook. A little judicious guidance had transferred the uncomfortable visitor to Olifant's hen-house. But they were not yet quite sure that he had been properly looked after. So for the present they gave up using the ground-holes, which were, of course, dangerous blind-alleys, and stuck closer than ever to the briers and the brush-piles that were left.

That first snow had quite gone and the weather was bright and warm until now. Molly, feeling a touch of rheumatism, was somewhere in the lower thicket seeking a tea-berry tonic. Rag was sitting in the weak sun-light on a bank in the east side. The smoke from the familiar gable chimney of Olifant's house came fitfully drifting a pale blue haze through the underwoods and showing as a dull brown against the brightness of the sky. The sun-gilt gable was cut off midway by the banks of brier-brush, that purple in shadow shone like rods of blazing crimson and gold in the light. Beyond the house the barn with its gable and roof, new gilt as the house, stood up like a Noah's ark.

The sounds that came from it, and yet more the delicious smell that mingled with the smoke, told Rag that the animals were being fed cabbage in the yard. Rag's mouth watered at the idea of the feast. He blinked and blinked

as he snuffed its odorous promises, for he loved
cabbage dearly. But then he had been to the
barnyard the night before after a few paltry
clover-tops, and no wise rabbit would go two
nights running to the same place.

Therefore he did the wise thing. He moved
across where he could not smell the cabbage
and made his supper of a bundle of hay that
had been blown from the stack. Later, when
about to settle for the night, he was joined by
Molly, who had taken her teaberry and then
eaten her frugal meal of sweet birch near the
Sunning Bank.

Meanwhile the sun had gone about his business elsewhere, taking all his gold and glory
with him. Off in the east a big black shutter
came pushing up and rising higher and higher;
it spread over the whole sky, shut out all light,
and left the world a very gloomy place indeed.
Then another mischief-maker, the wind, taking
advantage of the sun's absence, came on the
scene and set about brewing trouble. The
weather turned colder and colder; it seemed
worse than when the ground had been covered
with snow.

"Isn't this terribly cold? How I wish we
had our stove-pipe brush-pile," said Rag.

"A good night for the pine-root hole," replied Molly, "but we have not yet seen the pelt of that mink on the end of the barn, and it is not safe till we do."

The hollow hickory was gone—in fact at this very moment its trunk, lying in the wood-yard, was harboring the mink they feared. So the Cottontails hopped to the south side of the pond and, choosing a brush-pile, they crept under and snuggled down for the night, facing the wind but with their noses in different directions so as to go out different ways in case of alarm. The wind blew harder and colder as the hours went by, and about midnight a fine, icy snow came ticking down on the dead leaves and hissing through the brush heap. It might seem a poor night for hunting, but that old fox from Springfield was out. He came pointing up the wind in the shelter of the Swamp and chanced in the lee of the brush-pile, where he scented the sleeping Cottontails. He halted for a moment, then came stealthily sneaking up toward the brush under which his nose told him the rabbits were crouching. The noise of the wind and the sleet enabled him to come quite close before Molly heard the faint crunch of a dry leaf under his paw. She touched Rag's whiskers, and both were fully awake just as the fox sprang on them; but they always slept with their legs ready for a jump. Molly darted out into the blinding storm. The fox missed his spring, but followed like a racer, while Rag dashed off to one side.

There was only one road for Molly; that was . straight up the wind, and bounding for her life she gained a little over the unfrozen mud that would not carry the fox, till she reached the margin of the pond. No chance to turn now, on she must go.

Splash! splash! through the weeds she went, then plunge into the deep water.

And plunge went the fox close behind. But it was too much for Reynard on such a night. He turned back, and Molly, seeing only one course, struggled through the reeds into the deep water and struck out for the other shore. But there was a strong headwind. The little waves, icy cold, broke over her head as she swam, and the water was full of snow that blocked her way like soft ice, or floating mud. The dark line of the other shore seemed far, far away, with perhaps the fox waiting for her there.

But she laid her ears flat to be out of the gale, and bravely put forth all her strength with wind and tide against her. After a long, weary swim in the cold water, she had nearly reached the farther reeds when a great mass of floating snow barred her road; then the wind on the bank made strange, fox-like sounds that robbed her of all force, and she was drifted far backward before she could get free from the floating bar.

Again she struck out, but slowly—oh so slowly now. And when at last she reached the lee of the tall reeds, her limbs were numbed, her strength spent, her brave little heart was sinking, and she cared no more whether the fox were there or not. Through the reeds she did indeed pass, but once in the weeds her course wavered and slowed, her feeble strokes no longer sent her landward, and the ice forming around her, stopped her altogether. In a little while the cold, weak limbs ceased to move, the furry nose-tip of the little mother Cottontail wobbled no more, and the soft brown eyes were closed in death.

But there was no fox waiting to tear her with ravenous jaws. Rag had escaped the first onset of the foe, and as soon as he regained his wits he came running back to change-off and so help his mother. He met the old fox going round the pond to meet Molly and led him far and away, then dismissed him with a barbed·

wire gash on his head, and came to the bank
and sought about and trailed and thumped, but
all his searching was in vain; he could not find
his little mother. He never saw her again,
and never knew whither she went, for she slept
her never-waking sleep in the ice-arms of her
friend the Water that tells no tales.

Poor little Molly Cottontail! She was a true
heroine, yet only one of unnumbered millions
that without a thought of heroism have lived
and done their best in their little world, and
died. She fought a good fight in the battle of
life. She was good stuff; the stuff that never
dies. For flesh of her flesh and brain of her
brain was Rag She lives in him, and through
him transmits a finer fibre to her race.

And Rag still lives in the Swamp. Old Olifant died that winter, and the unthrifty sons
ceased to clear the Swamp or mend the wire
fences. Within a single year it was a wilder
place than ever; fresh trees and brambles
grew, and falling wires made many Cottontail
castles and last retreats that dogs and foxes
dared not storm. And there to this day lives
Rag. He is a big, strong buck now and fears
no rivals. He has a large family of his own,
and a pretty brown wife that he got no one
knows where. There, no doubt, he and his

children's children will flourish for many years to come, and there you may see them any sunny evening if you have learnt their signal code, and choosing a good spot on the ground, know just how and when to thump it.

VIXEN

THE SPRINGFIELD FOX

'And the little ones picked his Bones e·oh!'

VIXEN

THE SPRINGFIELD FOX

I

THE hens had been mysteriously disappearing for over a month; and when I came home to Springfield for the summer holidays it was my duty to find the cause. This was soon done. The fowls were carried away bodily one at a time, before going to roost, or else after leaving, which put tramps and neighbors out of court; they were not taken from the high perches, which cleared all coons and owls; or left partly eaten, so that weasels, skunks, or minks were not the guilty ones, and the blame, therefore, was surely left at Reynard's door.

The great pine wood of Erindale was on the other bank of the river, and on looking carefully about the lower ford I saw a few fox-tracks and a barred feather from one of our Plymouth Rock chickens. On climbing the farther bank in search of more clews, I heard a great outcry of crows behind me, and turning, saw a number of these birds darting down at something in the ford. A better view showed that it was the old story, thief catch thief, for there in the middle of the ford was a fox with something in his jaws—he was returning from our barnyard with another hen. The crows, though shameless robbers themselves, are ever first to cry 'Stop thief,' and yet more than ready to take 'hush-money' in the form of a share in the plunder.

And this was their game now. The fox to get back home must cross the river, where he was exposed to the full brunt of the crow mob. He made a dash for it, and would doubtless have gotten across with his booty had I not joined in the attack, whereupon he dropped the hen, scarce dead, and disappeared in the woods.

This large and regular levy of provisions wholly carried off could mean but one thing, a family of little foxes at home; and to find them I now was bound.

That evening I went with Ranger, my hound, across the river into the Erindale woods. As soon as the hound began to circle, we heard the short, sharp bark of a fox from a thickly wooded ravine close by. Ranger dashed in at once, struck a hot scent and went off on a lively straight-away till his voice was lost in the distance away over the upland.

After nearly an hour he came back, panting and warm, for it was baking August weather, and lay down at my feet.

But almost immediately the same foxy '*Yap yurrr*' was heard close at hand and off dashed the dog on another chase.

Away he went in the darkness, baying like a foghorn, straight away to the north. And the loud '*Boo, boo*,' became a low '*oo, oo*,' and that a feeble ' o-o ' and then was lost. They must have gone some miles away, for even with ear to the ground I heard nothing of them, though a mile was easy distance for Ranger's brazen voice.

As I waited in the black woods I heard a sweet sound of dripping water: '*Tink tank tenk tink, Ta tink tank tenk tonk.*'

I did not know of any spring so near, and in the hot night it was a glad find. But the sound led me to the bough of an oak-tree, where I found its source. Such a soft, sweet song; full of delightful suggestion on such a night:

Tonk tank tenk tink
Ta tink a tonk a tank a tink a
Ta ta tink tank ta ta tonk tink
Drink a tank a drink a drunk.

It was the 'water-dripping' song of the saw-whet owl.

But suddenly a deep raucous breathing and a rustle of leaves showed that Ranger was back. He was completely fagged out. His tongue hung almost to the ground and was dripping with foam, his flanks were heaving and spume-flecks dribbled from his breast and sides. He stopped panting a moment to give my hand a dutiful lick, then flung himself flop on the leaves to drown all other sounds with his noisy panting.

But again that tantalizing ' *Yap yurrr* ' was heard a few feet away, and the meaning of it all dawned on me.

We were close to the den where the little foxes were, and the old ones were taking turns in trying to lead us away.

It was late night now, so we went home feeling sure that the problem was nearly solved.

II

It was well known that there was an old fox with his family living in the neighborhood, but no one supposed them so near.

This fox had been called 'Scarface,' because of a scar reaching from his eye through and back of his ear ; this was supposed to have been given him by a barbed-wire fence during a rabbit hunt, and as the hair came in white after it healed, it was always a strong mark.

The winter before I had met with him and had had a sample of his craftiness. I was out shooting, after a fall of snow, and had crossed the open fields to the edge of the brushy hollow back of the old mill. As my head rose to a view of the hollow I caught sight of a fox trotting at long range down the other side, in line to cross my course. Instantly I held motionless, and did not even lower or turn my head lest I should catch his eye by moving, until he went on out of sight in the thick cover at the bottom. As soon as he was hidden I bobbed down and ran to head him off where he should leave the cover on the other side, and was there in good time awaiting, but no fox came forth. A careful look showed the fresh track of a fox that had bounded from the cover, and following it with my eye I saw old Scarface himself far out of range behind me, sitting on his haunches and grinning as though much amused.

A study of the trail made all clear. He had seen me at the moment I saw him, but he, also like a true hunter, had concealed the fact, putting on an air of unconcern till out of sight, when he had run for his life around behind me and amused himself by watching my stillborn trick.

In the springtime I had yet another instance of Scarface's cunning. I was walking with a friend along the road over the high pasture. We passed within thirty feet of a ridge on which were several gray and brown bowlders. When at the nearest point my friend said:

" Stone number three looks to me very much like a fox curled up."

But I could not see it, and we passed. We had not gone many yards farther when the wind blew on this bowlder as on fur.

My friend said, " I am sure that is a fox, lying asleep."

" We'll soon settle that," I replied, and turned back, but as soon as I had taken one step from the road, up jumped Scarface, for it was he, and ran. A fire had swept the middle of the pasture, leaving a broad belt of black; over this he skurried till he came to the unburnt yellow grass again, where he squatted down and was lost to view. He had been watching us all the time, and would not have moved had we kept to the road. The wonderful part of this is, not that he resembled the round stones and dry grass, but that he *knew he did*, and was ready to profit by it.

We soon found that it was Scarface and his wife Vixen that had made our woods their home and our barnyard their base of supplies.

Next morning a search in the pines showed a great bank of earth that had been scratched up within a few months. It must have come from a hole, and yet there was none to be seen. It is well known that a really cute fox, on digging a new den, brings all the earth out at the first hole made, but carries on a tunnel into some distant thicket. Then closing up for good the first made and too well-marked door, uses only the entrance hidden in the thicket.

So after a little search at the other side of a knoll, I found the real entry and good proof that there was a nest of little foxes inside.

Rising above the brush on the hillside was a great hollow basswood. It leaned a good deal and had a large hole at the bottom, and a smaller one at top.

We boys had often used this tree in playing Swiss Family Robinson, and by cutting steps in its soft punky walls had made it easy to go up and down in the hollow. Now it came in handy, for next day when the sun was warm I went there to watch, and from this perch on the roof, I soon saw the interesting family that lived in the cellar near by. There were four

little foxes; they looked curiously like little
lambs, with their woolly coats, their long, thick
legs and innocent expressions, and yet a second
glance at their broad, sharp-nosed, sharp-eyed
visages showed that each of these innocents
was the makings of a crafty old fox.

They played about, basking in the sun, or
wrestling with each other till a slight sound
made them skurry under ground. But their
alarm was needless, for the cause of it was their
mother; she stepped from the bushes bringing
another hen—number seventeen as I remember.
A low call from her and the little fellows came
tumbling out. Then began a scene that I
thought charming, but which my uncle would
not have enjoyed at all.

They rushed on the hen, and tussled and
fought with it, and each other, while the
mother, keeping a sharp eye for enemies,
looked on with fond delight. The expression
on her face was remarkable. It was first a
grinning of delight, but her usual look of wild-
ness and cunning was there, nor were cruelty
and nervousness lacking, but over all was the
unmistakable look of the mother's pride and
love.

The base of my tree was hidden in bushes
and much lower than the knoll where the den

They tussled and fought while their mother looked on with fond delight.

was. So I could come and go at will without scaring the foxes.

For many days I went there and saw much of the training of the young ones. They early learned to turn to statuettes at any strange sound, and then on hearing it again or finding other cause for fear, to run for shelter.

Some animals have so much mother-love that it overflows and benefits outsiders. Not so old Vixen it would seem. Her pleasure in the cubs led to most refined cruelty. For she often brought home to them mice and birds alive, and with diabolical gentleness would avoid doing them serious hurt so that the cubs might have larger scope to torment them.

There was a woodchuck that lived over in the hill orchard. He was neither handsome nor interesting, but he knew how to take care of himself. He had digged a den between the roots of an old pine-stump, so that the foxes could not follow him by digging. But hard work was not their way of life; wits they believed worth more than elbow-grease. This woodchuck usually sunned himself on the stump each morning. If he saw a fox near he went down in the door of his den, or if the enemy was very near he went inside and stayed long enough for the danger to pass.

One morning Vixen and her mate seemed to decide that it was time the children knew something about the broad subject of Woodchucks, and further that this orchard woodchuck would serve nicely for an object-lesson. So they went together to the orchard-fence unseen by old Chuckie on his stump. Scarface then showed himself in the orchard and quietly walked in a line so as to pass by the stump at a distance, but never once turned his head or allowed the ever-watchful woodchuck to think himself seen. When the fox entered the field the woodchuck quietly dropped down to the mouth of his den; here he waited as the fox passed, but concluding that after all wisdom is the better part, went into his hole.

This was what the foxes wanted. Vixen had kept out of sight, but now ran swiftly to the stump and hid behind it. Scarface had kept straight on, going very slowly. The woodchuck had not been frightened, so before long his head popped up between the roots and he looked around. There was that fox still going on, farther and farther away. The woodchuck grew bold as the fox went, and came out farther, and then seeing the coast clear, he scrambled onto the stump, and with one spring Vixen had him and shook him till he lay senseless. Scarface had watched out of the corner of his eye and now came running back. But Vixen took the chuck in her jaws and made for the den, so he saw he wasn't needed.

Back to the den came Vix, and carried the chuck so carefully that he was able to struggle a little when she got there. A low '*woof*' at the den brought the little fellows out like school-boys to play. She threw the wounded animal to them and they set on him like four little furies, uttering little growls and biting little bites with all the strength of their baby jaws, but the woodchuck fought for his life and beating them off slowly hobbled to the shelter of a thicket. The little ones pursued like a pack of hounds and dragged at his tail and flanks, but could not hold him back. So Vix overtook him with a couple of bounds and dragged him again into the open for the children to worry. Again and again this rough sport went on till one of the little ones was badly bitten, and his squeal of pain roused Vix to end the wood-chuck's misery and serve him up at once.

Not far from the den was a hollow overgrown with coarse grass, the playground of a colony of field-mice. The earliest lesson in woodcraft that the little ones took, away from the den, was in this hollow. Here they had their first course of mice, the easiest of all game. In teaching, the main thing was example, aided by a deep-set instinct. The old fox, also, had one or two signs meaning "lie still and watch," " come, do as I do," and so on, that were much used.

So the merry lot went to this hollow one calm evening and Mother Fox made them lie still in the grass. Presently a faint squeak showed that the game was astir. Vix rose up and went on tip-toe into the grass—not crouching, but as high as she could stand, sometimes on her hind legs so as to get a better view. The runs that the mice follow are hidden under the grass tangle, and the only way to know the whereabouts of a mouse is by seeing the slight shaking of the grass, which is the reason why mice are hunted only on calm days.

And the trick is to locate the mouse and seize him first and see him afterward. Vix soon made a spring, and in the middle of the bunch of dead grass that she grabbed was a field-mouse squeaking his last squeak.

He was soon gobbled, and the four awkward little foxes tried to do the same as their mother, and when at length the eldest for the first time in his life caught game, he quivered with excitement and ground his pearly little milk-teeth

into the mouse with a rush of inborn savageness that must have surprised even himself.

Another home lesson was on the red-squirrel. One of these noisy, vulgar creatures, lived
close by and used to waste part of each day
scolding the foxes, from some safe perch. The
cubs made many vain attempts to catch him as
he ran across their glade from one tree to another, or spluttered and scolded at them a foot
or so out of reach. But old Vixen was up in
natural history—she knew squirrel nature and
took the case in hand when the proper time
came. She hid the children and lay down flat
in the middle of the open glade. The saucy
low-minded squirrel came and scolded as usual.
But she moved no hair. He came nearer and
at last right overhead to chatter :

" You brute you, you brute you."

But Vix lay as dead. This was very per-
plexing, so the squirrel came down the trunk
and peeping about made a nervous dash across
the grass, to another tree, again to scold from
a safe perch.

" You brute you, you useless brute, scarrr-
scarrrrr."

But flat and lifeless on the grass lay Vix.
This was most tantalizing to the squirrel. He
was naturally curious and disposed to be vent-

uresome, so again he came to the ground and skurried across the glade nearer than before.

Still as death lay Vix, " surely she was dead." And the little foxes began to wonder if their mother wasn't asleep.

But the squirrel was working himself into a little craze of foolhardy curiosity. He had dropped a piece of bark on Vix's head ; he had used up his list of bad words, and he had done it all over again, without getting a sign of life. So after a couple more dashes across the glade he ventured within a few feet of the really watchful Vix, who sprang to her feet and pinned him in a twinkling.

" And the little ones picked the bones e-oh."

Thus the rudiments of their education were laid, and afterward, as they grew stronger, they were taken farther afield to begin the higher branches of trailing and scenting.

For each kind of prey they were taught a way to hunt, for every animal has some great strength or it could not live, and some great weakness or the others could not live. The squirrel's weakness was foolish curiosity ; the fox s that he can't climb a tree. And the training of the little foxes was all shaped to take advantage of the weakness of the other creatures and to make up for their own by defter play where they are strong.

From their parents they learned the chief axioms of the fox world. How, is not easy to say. But that they learned this in company with their parents was clear. Here are some that foxes taught me, without saying a word:—

Never sleep on your straight track.

Your nose is before your eyes, then trust it first.

A fool runs down the wind.

Running rills cure many ills.

Never take the open if you can keep the cover.

Never leave a straight trail if a crooked one will do.

If it's strange, it's hostile.

Dust and water burn the scent.

Never hunt mice in a rabbit-woods, or rabbits in a henyard.

Keep off the grass.

Inklings of the meanings of these were already entering the little ones' minds — thus, 'Never follow what you can't smell,' was wise, they could see, because if you can't smell it, then the wind is so that it must smell you.

One by one they learned the birds and beasts of their home woods, and then as they were able to go abroad with their parents they learned new animals. They were beginning to think they knew the scent of everything that moved. But one night the mother took them to a field where was a strange black flat thing on the ground. She brought them on purpose to smell it, but at the first whiff their every hair stood on end, they trembled, they knew not why—it seemed to tingle through their blood and fill them with instinctive hate and fear. And when she saw its full effect she told them—

" *That is man-scent.*"

III

Meanwhile the hens continued to disappear. I had not betrayed the den of cubs. Indeed, I thought a good deal more of the little rascals than I did of the hens; but uncle was dreadfully wrought up and made most disparaging remarks about my woodcraft. To please him

I one day took the hound across to the woods and seating myself on a stump on the open hillside, I bade the dog go on. Within three minutes he sang out in the tongue all hunters know so well, " Fox! fox! ᶠox! straight away down the valley."

After awhile I heard them coming back. There I saw the fox—Scarface—loping lightly across the river-bottom to the stream. In he went and trotted along in the shallow water near the margin for two hundred yards, then came out straight toward me. Though in full view, he saw me not, but came up the hill watching over his shoulder for the hound. Within ten feet of me he turned and sat with his back to me while he craned his neck and showed an eager interest in the doings of the hound. Ranger came bawling along the trail till he came to the running water, the killer of scent, and here he was puzzled; but there was only one thing to do; that was by going up and down both banks find where the fox had left the river.

The fox before me shifted his position a little to get a better view and watched with a most human interest all the circling of the hound. He was so close that I saw the hair of his shoulder bristle a little when the dog came in sight. I could see the jumping of his heart on his ribs, and the gleam of his yellow eye. When the dog was wholly baulked by the water trick it was comical to see:—he could not sit still, but rocked up and down in glee, and reared on his hind feet to get a better view of the slow-plodding hound. With mouth opened nearly to his ears, though not at all winded, he panted noisily for a moment, or rather he laughed gleefully just as a dog laughs by grinning and panting.

Old Scarface wriggled in huge enjoyment as the hound puzzled over the trail so long that when he did find it, it was so stale he could barely follow it, and did not feel justified in tonguing on it at all.

As soon as the hound was working up the hill, the fox quietly went into the woods. I had been sitting in plain view only ten feet away, but I had the wind and kept still and the fox never knew that his life had for twenty minutes been in the power of the foe he most feared. Ranger would also have passed me as near as the fox, but I spoke to him, and with a little nervous start he quit the trail and looking sheepish lay down by my feet.

This little comedy was played with variations

for several days, but it was all in plain view from the house across the river. My uncle, impatient at the daily loss of hens, went out himself, sat on the open knoll, and when old Scarface trotted to his lookout to watch the dull hound on the river flat below, my uncle remorselessly shot him in the back, at the very moment when he was grinning over a new triumph.

IV

But still the hens were disappearing. My uncle was wrathy. He determined to conduct the war himself, and sowed the woods with poison baits, trusting to luck that our own dogs would not get them. He indulged in contemptuous remarks on my by-gone woodcraft, and went out evenings with a gun and the two dogs, to see what he could destroy.

Vix knew right well what a poison bait was ; she passed them by or else treated them with active contempt, but one she dropped down the hole of an old enemy, a skunk, who was never afterward seen. Formerly old Scarface was always ready to take charge of the dogs, and keep them out of mischief. But now that Vix had the whole burden of the brood, she could no longer spend time in breaking every track to the den, and was not always at hand to meet and mislead the foes that might be coming too near.

The end is easily foreseen. Ranger followed a hot trail to the den, and Spot, the fox-terrier, announced that the family was at home, and then did his best to go in after them.

The whole secret was now out, and the whole family doomed. The hired man came around with pick and shovel to dig them out, while we and the dogs stood by. Old Vix soon showed herself in the near woods, and led the dogs away off down the river, where she shook them off when she thought proper, by the simple device of springing on a sheep's back. The frightened animal ran for several hundred yards; then Vix got off, knowing that there was now a hopeless gap in the scent, and returned to the den. But the dogs, baffled by the break in the trail, soon did the same, to find Vix hanging about in despair, vainly trying to decoy us away from her treasures.

Meanwhile Paddy plied both pick and shovel with vigor and effect. The yellow, gravelly sand was heaping on both sides, and the shoulders of the sturdy digger were sinking below the level. After an hour's digging, enlivened by frantic rushes of the dogs after the old fox, who hovered near in the woods, Pat called:

"Here they are, sor!"

It was the den at the end of the burrow, and cowering as far back as they could, were the four little woolly cubs.

Before I could interfere, a murderous blow from the shovel, and a sudden rush for the fierce little terrier, ended the lives of three. The fourth and smallest was barely saved by holding him by his tail high out of reach of the excited dogs.

He gave one short squeal, and his poor mother came at the cry, and circled so near that she would have been shot but for the accidental protection of the dogs, who somehow always seemed to get between, and whom she once more led away on a fruitless chase.

The little one saved alive was dropped into a bag, where he lay quite still. His unfortunate brothers were thrown back into their nursery bed, and buried under a few shovelfuls of earth.

We guilty ones then went back into the house, and the little fox was soon chained in the yard. No one knew just why he was kept alive, but in all a change of feeling had set in, and the idea of killing him was without a supporter.

He was a pretty little fellow, like a cross between a fox and a lamb. His woolly visage and form were strangely lamb-like and innocent, but one could find in his yellow eyes a gleam of cunning and savageness as unlamb-like as it possibly could be.

As long as anyone was near he crouched sullen and cowed in his shelter-box, and it was a full hour after being left alone before he ventured to look out.

My window now took the place of the hollow basswood. A number of hens of the breed he knew so well were about the cub in the yard. Late that afternoon as they strayed near the captive there was a sudden rattle of the chain, and the youngster dashed at the nearest one and would have caught him but for the chain which brought him up with a jerk. He got on his feet and slunk back to his box, and though he afterward made several rushes he so gauged his leap as to win or fail within the length of the chain and never again was brought up by its cruel jerk.

As night came down the little fellow became very uneasy, sneaking out of his box, but going back at each slight alarm, tugging at his chain, or at times biting it in fury while he held it down with his fore-paws. Suddenly he paused as though listening, then raising h's little black nose he poured out a short, quavering cry.

Once or twice this was repeated, the time between being occupied in worrying the chain and running about. Then an answer came. The far-away *Yap yurrr* of the old fox. A few minutes later a shadowy form appeared on the wood-pile. The little one slunk into his box, but at once returned and ran to meet his mother with all the gladness that a fox could show. Quick as a flash she seized him and turned to bear him away by the road she came. But the moment the end of the chain was reached the cub was rudely jerked from the old one's mouth, and she, scared by the opening of a window, fled over the wood-pile.

An hour afterward the cub had ceased to run about or cry. I peeped out, and by the light of the moon saw the form of the mother at full length on the ground by the little one gnawing at something—the clank of iron told what, it was that cruel chain. And Tip, the little one, meanwhile was helping himself to a warm drink.

On my going out she fled into the dark woods, but there by the shelter-box were two little mice, bloody and still warm, food for the cub brought by the devoted mother. And in the morning I found the chain was very bright for a foot or two next the little one's collar.

On walking across the woods to the ruined den, I again found signs of Vixen. The poor heart-broken mother had come and dug out the bedraggled bodies of her little ones.

There lay the three little baby foxes all licked smooth now, and by them were two of our hens fresh killed. The newly heaved earth was printed all over with tell-tale signs—signs that told me that here by the side of her dead she had watched like Rizpah. Here she had brought their usual meal, the spoil of her nightly hunt. Here she had stretched herself beside them and vainly offered them their natural drink and yearned to feed and warm them as of old; but only stiff little bodies under their soft wool she found, and little cold noses still and unresponsive.

A deep impress of elbows, breast, and hocks showed where she had laid in silent grief and watched them for long and mourned as a wild mother can mourn for its young. But from that time she came no more to the ruined den, for now she surely knew that her little ones were dead.

V

Tip, the captive, the weakling of the brood, was now the heir to all her love. The dogs were loosed to guard the hens. The hired man had orders to shoot the old fox on sight—so had I, but was resolved never to see her. Chicken-heads, that a fox loves and a dog will not touch, had been poisoned and scattered through the woods; and the only way to the yard where Tip was tied was by climbing the wood-pile after braving all other dangers. And yet each night old Vix was there to nurse her baby and bring it fresh-killed hens and game. Again and again I saw her, although she came now without awaiting the querulous cry of the captive.

The second night of the captivity I heard the rattle of the chain, and then made out that the old fox was there, hard at work digging a hole by the little one's kennel. When it was deep enough to half bury her, she gathered into it all the slack of the chain, and filled it again with earth. Then in triumph thinking she had gotten rid of the chain, she seized little Tip by the neck and turned to dash off up the wood-pile, but alas only to have him jerked roughly from her grasp.

Poor little fellow, he whimpered sadly as he crawled into his box. After half an hour there was a great outcry among the dogs, and by their straight-away tonguing through the far woods I knew they were chasing Vix. Away up north they went in the direction of the railway and their noise faded from hearing. Next morning the hound had not come back. We soon knew why. Foxes long ago learned what a railroad is; they soon devised several ways of turning it to account. One way is when hunted to walk the rails for a long distance just before a train comes. The scent, always poor on iron, is destroyed by the train and there is always a chance of hounds being killed by the engine. But another way more sure, but harder to play, is to lead the hounds straight to a high trestle just ahead of the train, so that the engine overtakes them on it and they are surely dashed to destruction.

This trick was skilfully played, and down below we found the mangled remains of old Ranger and learned that Vix was already wreaking her revenge.

That same night she returned to the yard before Spot's weary limbs could bring him back and killed another hen and brought it to Tip, and stretched her panting length beside him that he might quench his thirst. For she seemed to think he had no food but what she brought.

It was that hen that betrayed to my uncle the nightly visits.

My own sympathies were all turning to Vix, and I would have no hand in planning further murders. Next night my uncle himself watched, gun in hand, for an hour. Then when it became cold and the moon clouded over he remembered other important business elsewhere, and left Paddy in his place.

But Paddy was "onaisy" as the stillness and anxiety of watching worked on his nerves. And the loud bang! bang! an hour later left us sure only that powder had been burned.

In the morning we found Vix had not failed her young one. Again next night found my uncle on guard, for another hen had been taken. Soon after dark a single shot was heard, but Vix dropped the game she was bringing and escaped. Another attempt made that night called forth another gun-shot. Yet next day it was seen by the brightness of the chain that she had come again and vainly tried for hours to cut that hateful bond.

Such courage and stanch fidelity were bound

to win respect, if not toleration. At any rate, there was no gunner in wait next night, when all was still. Could it be of any use? Driven off thrice with gun-shots, would she make another try to feed or free her captive young one?

Would she? Hers was a mother's love. There was but one to watch them this time, the fourth night, when the quavering whine of the little one was followed by that shadowy form above the wood-pile.

But carrying no fowl or food that could be seen. Had the keen huntress failed at last? Had she no head of game for this her only charge, or had she learned to trust his captors for his food?

No, far from all this. The wild-wood mother's heart and hate were true. Her only thought had been to set him free. All means she knew she tried, and every danger braved to tend him well and help him to be free. But all had failed.

Like a shadow she came and in a moment was gone, and Tip seized on something dropped, and crunched and chewed with relish what she brought. But even as he ate, a knife-like pang shot through and a scream of pain escaped him. Then there was a momentary struggle and the little fox was dead.

The mother's love was strong in Vix, but a higher thought was stronger. She knew right well the poison's power; she knew the poison bait, and would have taught him had he lived to know and shun it too. But now at last when she must choose for him a wretched prisoner's life or sudden death, she quenched the mother in her breast and freed him by the one remaining door.

. . . .

It is when the snow is on the ground that we take the census of the woods, and when the winter came it told me that Vix no longer roamed the woods of Erindale. Where she went it never told, but only this, that she was gone.

Gone, perhaps, to some other far-off haunt to leave behind the sad remembrance of her murdered little ones and mate. Or gone, may be, deliberately, from the scene of a sorrowful life, as many a wild-wood mother has gone, by the means that she herself had used to free her young one, the last of all her brood.